THE PROBABILITY
OF LOVE

What Reviewers Say About Dena Blake's Work

Love By Proxy

"Brilliantly Funny and Sweet! ...This was such an amazing story! Gripping, exciting, full of twists and turns, unexpected events, and most importantly a little touch of comedy. It really was the perfect rom-com. Packed with drama and lots of conflict, nothing was more exhilarating then being on this rollercoaster of emotions with Tess and Sophie."—*LESBIreviewed*

Next Exit Home

"I enjoy Dena Blake's writing, and I enjoyed this book a lot. ...I especially liked this book because the two single mums who have become mums for very different reasons/experiences are strong women. Proving they are super capable to solo parent and raise rockstar kids. There is something very sexy about a single mum grabbing parenthood by the horns and making it work. I really enjoyed that aspect! ...Great small-town romance that packs a punch in the enemies to lovers trope! I'll definitely be rereading this one again soon."—*Les Rêveur*

Kiss Me Every Day

"This book was SUCH a fun read!! ...This was such a fun, interesting book to read and I thoroughly enjoyed it; the characters were super easy to like, the romance was super cute and I loved seeing each little thing that Wynn changed every day!"—*Sasha & Amber Read*

"Such a fun and an exciting book filled with so much love! This book is just packed with fun and memorable moments I was thinking about for days after reading it. This is one hundred per cent my new favourite Dena Blake book. The pace of the book was excellent, and I felt I was along for the fantastic ride."—*Les Rêveur*

"The sweetest moment in the book is when the titular phrase is uttered. ...This well written book is an interesting read because of the whole premise of getting repeated opportunities to right wrongs." —*Best Lesfic Reviews*

"Wynn's journey of self-discovery is wonderful to witness. She develops compassion, love and finds happiness. Her character development is phenomenal. ...If you're looking for a stunning romance book with a female/female romance, then this is definitely the one for you. I highly recommend."—*Literatureaesthetic*

Perfect Timing

"The chemistry between Lynn and Maggie is fantastic...the writing is totally engrossing."—*Best Lesfic Reviews*

"This book is the kind of book you sit down to on a Sunday morning with a cup of tea and the sun shining in your bedroom only to realise at 5 pm you've not left your bed because it was too good to stop reading."—*Les Rêveur*

"The relationship between Lynn and Maggie developed at a organic pace. I loved all the flirting going on between Maggie and Lynn. I love a good flirty conversation! ...I haven't read this author before but I look forward to trying more of her titles."—Marcia Hull, Librarian (Ponca City Library, Oklahoma)

Racing Hearts

"I particularly liked Drew with her sexy rough exterior and soft heart. ...Sex scenes are definitely getting hotter and I think this might be the hottest by Dena Blake to date..."—*Les Rêveur*

Just One Moment

"One of the things I liked is that the story is set after the glorious days of falling in love, after the time when everything is exciting. It

shows how sometimes, trying to make life better really makes it more complicated. ...It's also, and mainly, a reminder of how important communication is between partners, and that as solid as trust seems between two lovers, misunderstandings happen very easily."
—*Jude in the Stars*

"Blake does angst particularly well and she's wrung every possible ounce out of this one. ...I found myself getting sucked right into the story—I do love a good bit of angst and enjoy the copious amounts of drama on occasion."—*C-Spot Reviews*

Friends Without Benefits

"This is the book when the Friends to Lovers trope doesn't work out. When you tell your best friend you are in love with her and she doesn't return your feelings. This book is real life and I think I loved it more for that..."—*Les Rêveur*

A Country Girl's Heart

"Dena Blake just goes from strength to strength."—*Les Rêveur*

"Literally couldn't put this book down, and can't give enough praise for how good this was!!! One of my favourite reads, and I highly recommend to anyone who loves a fantastically clever, intriguing, and exciting romance."—*LESBIreviewed*

Unchained Memories

"There is a lot of angst and the book covers some difficult topics but it does that well. The writing is gripping and the plot flows."
—Melina Bickard, Librarian, Waterloo Library (UK)

"This story had me cycling between lovely romantic scenes to white-knuckle gripping, on the edge of the seat (or in my case, the bed) scenarios. This story had me rooting for a sequel and I can certainly place my stamp of approval on this novel as a must read book."
—*Lesbian Review*

"The pace and character development was perfect for such an involved story line, I couldn't help but turn each page. This book has so many wonderful plot twists that you will be in suspense with every chapter that follows."—*Les Rêveur*

Where the Light Glows

"From first time author, Dena Blake, *Where the Light Glows* is a sure winner..."—*A Bookworm's Loft*

"[T]he vivid descriptions of the Pacific Northwest will make readers hungry for food and travel. The chemistry between Mel and Izzy is palpable..."—*RT Book Reviews*

"I'm still shocked this was Dena Blake's first novel. ...It was fantastic. ...It was written extremely well and more than once I wondered if this was a true account of someone close to the author because it was really raw and realistic. It seemed to flow very naturally and I am truly surprised that this is the author's first novel as it reads like a seasoned writer..."—*Les Rêveur*

Visit us at www.boldstrokesbooks.com

By the Author

Where the Light Glows

Unchained Memories

A Country Girl's Heart

Racing Hearts

Friends Without Benefits

Just One Moment

Perfect Timing

Kiss Me Every Day

Next Exit Home

Love By Proxy

The Probability Of Love

THE PROBABILITY OF LOVE

by

Dena Blake

2022

THE PROBABILITY OF LOVE

ISBN 13: 978-1-63679-188-3

THIS TRADE PAPERBACK ORIGINAL IS PUBLISHED BY
BOLD STROKES BOOKS, INC.
P.O. BOX 249
VALLEY FALLS, NY 12185

FIRST EDITION: JULY 2022

CREDITS
EDITOR: SHELLEY THRASHER
PRODUCTION DESIGN: SUSAN RAMUNDO
COVER DESIGN BY JEANINE HENNING

Acknowledgments

We've all met people in our lives with whom we've taken chances…or that we wish we had. A leap of faith that leads to a friendship, a weekend fling, or a happily-ever-after. We know it when we feel it—that tingle, that rush of adrenaline, the euphoria of clicking with someone in so many ways. Life has given us many challenges over the past few years, so whether you take a chance on something new or not, enjoy what you have in life your own way.

Rad and Sandy—there's no one I trust my work with more than Bold Strokes Books. The support and care provided by the production crew is stellar. From when my first word hits the page until the book is released in print. Thanks to Shelley Thrasher, my editor extraordinaire, for being patient and persistent in teaching me how to be a better writer.

To my writing friends, you keep me motivated and sane. Thanks for listening, checking in, and making me laugh. We'll see each other soon.

To Kate—my other half—my person. If I've learned anything during the past few years, it's that we can survive in a world full of chaos and still become closer. Wes and Haley—you are STILL by far my best accomplishments in life.

Thank you to the readers out there who made time to read. I appreciate you all very much. You keep me writing.

Dedication

For all the risk takers out there.
Whether it's a message—a phone call—a night—
or a weekend—sometimes you win.

CHAPTER ONE

Rachel Taylor had almost finished working with her last patient of the morning when her phone buzzed in her pocket again. It had rung several times, and now it seemed a string of texts was coming through. Who was blowing up her phone? She needed to finish with her patient before she found out.

"I worked you pretty hard today, so you might be sore later." The patient had just begun therapy, due to rotator-cuff surgery. Rachel went to the sink, washed her hands, and dried them. "Take a couple of ibuprofen when you get home."

"Will do. Thanks, Doctor Taylor." He glanced over his shoulder as he walked to the door. "I didn't realize you had such a nice physical-therapy room here in the hospital."

"We keep it a secret. Only certain patients have access to our magic." She smiled as he left the room and then scanned the medium-sized room with wood floors spanning the space and mirrors covering several walls. There was no place else she'd rather work. It wasn't state of the art yet, but it included various types of equipment, including parallel bars, exercise steps, weights, recumbent bikes, and medicine balls, which were grouped in different stations around the room. The half-wall finished with a large plate-glass window spanning it just short of the ceiling separating the office area made the room seem a lot bigger than it was. She hoped to expand their equipment and move to a larger space soon.

As she headed into her office, she quickly tugged her phone from her back pocket to see who'd been blowing it up with messages. It was

Amy, the other main physical-therapy doctor in the department—her second in command. She read the messages that had come through in succession.

I have strep throat.

Can't go to the conference.

You'll have to go in my place. I booked your flight. It leaves at seven tonight.

I emailed you my presentation.

Rachel sank into a chair and hit the speed-dial button to call Amy. Her phone rang several times before going to voice mail.

She quickly typed in a message.

You're yanking my chain, right?

No. I'm serious. Can't talk. Lost my voice.

Her stomach dropped. "Shit." She certainly didn't need this today. It was First Friday at the gallery this week, and she was supposed to go with Shay. She'd been looking forward to it all week. But no way could she cancel the presentation in Las Vegas. Amy was scheduled to discuss some of the breakthrough therapy they'd been doing at the hospital. They'd worked on the presentation for months, and it was part of their plan to obtain more funding for the department. She'd just have to suck it up and go.

She glanced at her watch and then clicked a few keys on the computer to bring up her schedule. Her afternoon appointments would need to be rescheduled to another therapist or another day. She needed to get home and do some laundry—at least some jeans and underwear. Other than that, whatever shirts she had in her closet would have to do. Trying to curb her anxiety, she sucked in a deep breath. It usually took her weeks to mentally prepare to speak in front of a crowd, which she hadn't done in months. Lately she'd been letting Amy do most of the presenting, since it was shared research. She wasn't prepared to travel either—she wasn't ready for any of it.

She accessed her e-mail and sent the presentation and notes to the printer, as well as her boarding pass for the flight to Las Vegas Amy had booked. She'd start reviewing the information when she got settled on the plane. She wouldn't say exactly what Amy had included in her notes, but she didn't have time to change them now. She'd just have to wing it. The wheels on her chair creaked as she pushed back to stand and retrieve the documents from the printer. She reached for her laptop bag leaning against the wall behind her and checked to make sure the spare power cord was in one of the pockets before she slid the laptop and documents inside.

The phone rang. It was Meg at the reception desk. She picked up the receiver and immediately began to speak. "I need to leave early. Can you reschedule my appointments?"

"Already on it. Amy messaged me. Have a safe trip." Meg's voice was cheerful, as always.

"Great. Thanks."

"And try to have some fun while you're there."

"Not making any promises, but I'll do my best." She dropped the receiver into its cradle. What kind of fun could she possibly have by herself in the gaming capital of the US? Hopefully the hotel would have a good sports bar, where she could at least catch some interesting entertainment. She threw her bag over her shoulder and stepped out into the main room to let one of the other therapists know the situation before she went through the side door of the unit and headed to the elevator. She was sure she'd left something behind but couldn't think of anything else she needed from her office.

Outside, the heat hit her like a brick wall. The stifling heat in Florida always amazed her. Even so close to the Gulf in Tampa, it could be suffocating.

Once Rachel was in her car, she fired the engine and let the air conditioning blast the heat away. She would keep it on high until her face was frozen, to combat the sweat already gathering on the back of her neck. She secured her phone to the magnetic holder on her dash and hit the speed-dial button for Shay.

Shay answered right away. "Hey there. I was just trying to decide where we're going to grab dinner before the event tomorrow night." She sounded happy, and Rachel hated to spoil her mood.

"About that. I'm not going to be able to make it. I have to fly to Las Vegas tonight and give a presentation tomorrow."

"Seriously? That's kind of short notice, isn't it?"

"Yeah. Amy, my research partner, was planning to do it, but she's sick."

"Can't you cancel?"

"Not really. It's kind of a big deal. We'll get some great exposure. I'm sorry." She'd earn some accreditation hours for it as well.

"It's okay." Shay sounded disappointed. "Promise me you won't stay in the casino the whole time. See some of the not-so-commercialized places in Las Vegas while you're there."

"You want to come with me?"

"Wish I could, but Chloe would probably question that decision. Plus, you know I don't like to miss her events."

"Yeah. That would be bad." She slammed on the brakes hard when the car in front of her decided to stop at a yellow light. "I'll call you when I get home. Traffic's crazy."

"Okay. Sounds good."

Part of Shay's deal with Chloe when they got back together was that they would support each other in all their endeavors—no matter what. Rachel would've preferred a different outcome from their reconciliation, but it was selfish to hope that their relationship wouldn't work out and that Shay would be hers eventually. That thought still lurked in the back of her mind.

Once Rachel was home, she headed straight to the spare bedroom and searched for her carry-on. She hadn't used it in so long she couldn't remember exactly where it was. Not on the upper closet shelf. She dropped to her knees and looked under the bed—not there either. Finally, she found it in the back corner of the closet hidden by dresses she never wore anymore. She really needed to give them to someone who actually liked to wear them, but she'd kept them for random hospital functions.

She loaded her suitcase with the items on her packing list and threw in a couple of extra pairs of shorts and a few T-shirts just in case she was able to get out of the hotel. That would be the only good part about this last-minute trip. Maybe she could find someone at the conference to pal around with to do some less-touristy things.

CHAPTER TWO

Blair Haskell sat with her laptop open in one of the two chairs at the small, round dinette set in her kitchen adjusting a few numbers on the financial spreadsheet for her bartending business plan. Her website would come next, a task she wasn't looking forward to since she wasn't very good at HTML code. From her calculations, if she took on a few more shifts at the casino bar, she'd be able to move her timeline up and return home to Orlando sooner than she'd planned.

Las Vegas hadn't been her first choice when she'd decided to get out of Florida for a while, but it fit all the criteria. It was far enough away to put some distance between her and Tess, the woman she'd thought she had a shot with last summer, and it was a good place to earn some extra cash. Her aunt also lived here and had a house she could rent.

She'd been gone for close to a year—long enough to get over the sting of rejection. She was honestly happy that Tess had found her true love with Sophie. It had taken a while to become friendly with them, but Tess had persisted, and she finally realized Tess's intentions had been good, that she'd never meant to hurt her. In any case, she seemed to have been the catalyst that brought Tess and Sophie together, even if it was the most awkward situation she'd ever been involved in.

Her phone rang, and she checked the screen to see who was calling. It was Tess, of course. Who else would it be? It wasn't like she had many friends, at least none that checked up on her—actually called instead of texting. She hit the green button and put the phone on speaker.

"How's the planning going?" Tess's sweet, upbeat voice filled the room.

"It's not." She sighed.

"Why? What's wrong?"

"I'm just not in the mood to crunch numbers today. I need people interaction. Come have dinner with me?"

"Sure. I'll be right over." Tess laughed—that wonderful laugh of hers. "It'll be late though. You know, with the drive to the airport and the usual five-hour flight."

"You'd think someone would've invented the teleporter by now."

"Right? What are all the geniuses of the world working on anyway?" The phone muffled for a minute. "Sophie says hi."

"Hi back to her." She wasn't nearly as friendly with Sophie, but she came along with Tess's friendship.

"She wants to know when Morgan is moving back to Orlando."

"Not for a couple weeks, I think." Morgan was a friend who had also come to Las Vegas for the financial opportunity. While she was in town, she was staying with Blair. It seemed to be a good arrangement for them both. They'd been friends for a while, and previously Morgan had been bartending at the Palm Beach Resort when Blair first met Tess and Sophie.

"Tell her to wrap it up there. We'll need her here sooner than we thought."

Morgan was scheduled to start a business internship with Sophie and Tess's newly formed business next month—SoTess Marketing. Morgan certainly seemed to have her stuff together for someone in her mid-twenties. Much more than Blair did in her thirties.

"Really? Things must be ramping up for you pretty well then."

"They are. Apparently, our ads for Boho Clothes are getting noticed. We've gained a few more clients just in the last couple of weeks." Tess and Sophie had quit their previous positions at another firm and ventured out on their own about the same time Blair had moved to Vegas.

"That was a spectacular layout." The theme was magical, just like something out of a fairy tale.

"Well, thank you."

"Do you know anyone who can show me how to build a website?" She hoped Tess could help her out but didn't want to ask her directly.

"Me. Of course. I thought you'd never ask."

"I didn't want to presume." She was relieved Tess had offered. She didn't relish the thought of finding someone on her own.

"I've actually already started building something. Have you decided on a name yet?"

"I have a few knocking around, but I think I'll go with Blissful Bubbles." She'd made a list of ten and pared it down daily until that was the last one left.

"Ooh, I like it. I can do a lot with that. Champagne bottles, beer suds, sparkling water. So many choices."

"Don't outclass me. I want people to know I'm affordable."

"Don't worry about that. I'll make sure everyone knows how cheap you are." Tess laughed at herself. "I'll get you a link early next week."

"No rush. I'm sure you have something planned for the weekend." Tess and Sophie always did.

"I forgot to tell you. We're going to an art event. I've been dabbling in painting a bit, and my art will be on display tonight in Tampa."

"That's awesome. I had no idea you were interested in selling any of your works."

"I wasn't really. Sophie contacted the gallery owner and set it up as a surprise."

"That was sweet." A tad of jealousy seeped in again.

"Yeah. It really was." Tess sighed. "And to think you're responsible for getting us together."

"In a weird sort of way." She laughed. "You two would've figured it out sooner or later without me."

"You did it nonetheless." Her voice muffled again for a minute. "Hey. I have to go. Sophie fixed dinner tonight, and she's plating it now."

"Wow. That's unusual."

"It's a miracle. Call me tomorrow, and we can discuss more about the website."

"Will do. I can't wait to hear how dinner turned out." She ended the call.

Tess was the perfect woman—sweet, kind, and sexy in her own way. Blair had been disappointed by the whole weird situation that had brought them together. After all, Sophie was the one who had originally been communicating online with her, and the weekend at the Palm Beach Resort was supposed to be a romantic getaway for the two of them. She'd been caught off guard when Tess had shown up instead, then pleasantly surprised when she'd gotten to know her. But nothing worked out between them. Soon after she met Tess, Sophie had arrived, and it was clear that Tess only had eyes for Sophie and vice versa.

Blair hoped for something just as perfect someday, but currently her life was too busy for a romantic connection. Her heart wasn't ready for it either. Right now she wanted to earn enough money to get her bartending business off the ground. That took working two jobs and a lot of extra shifts, which left zero time for romance.

CHAPTER THREE

Rachel paid the cab driver and waited for him to pull her bag from the trunk. The conference hotel was one of the upper-scale hotels in Las Vegas. She paused to take in the flashing lights and neon colors that lit up the sky on the strip. You couldn't see such a spectacular sight anywhere else. She rolled her bag up the sidewalk and waved off the bellman when he offered to help her take it inside. It was late, and she didn't want to worry about whether her bag would get to her room. Bells and chimes filled her ears as she entered and passed the bank of slot machines located by the entrance, a sound she'd forgotten since the last time she was here. The check-in area, filled with tall, round pillars and a marble floor, was typical of a hotel of its caliber. The counter wasn't swamped, but it was busy enough that she'd have to wait, and with only two people working the counter, the line didn't seem to be moving quickly.

When she finally reached it, a woman with a cheerful smile greeted her. "Checking in?"

"Yes. I have a reservation." She slid the printed confirmation across the counter.

The woman clicked the keyboard furiously before she glanced up. "It looks like this room was cancelled."

"It wasn't cancelled. It should've been modified to add my name."

"May I see your driver's license, please?"

She took her ID from her bag and set it on the counter.

The woman glanced at it as she typed. "Was the reservation originally in your name?"

"No. It was made under Amy Baker, but she said she added me to the room reservation. She's unable to attend the conference."

"Give me just a second." The clerk continued to type without any change to her stoic expression.

"Listen. I've had a long flight. I'm tired, and I just need a room." Rachel was not at all happy. It was late, maybe not in Vegas with the three-hour time adjustment, but back home in Florida, it was after eleven o'clock. She just wanted to crawl into bed and sleep. Thankfully she didn't have to present until tomorrow afternoon, but she still needed to review and practice her presentation.

"I'm sorry, miss. There seems to have been a mix-up with your reservation. I've found you a room, but it will be about an hour until it's ready." She handed her a map of the hotel. "You can check your luggage at the bell desk until then, if you'd like. Maybe have a drink at one of the bars?"

"Thanks, but I'll keep my bag with me and be back in an hour." Just her luck. She didn't want a drink, just a nice, comfortable bed for the night, and she'd be happy. But no—not even that could go right. She grabbed the hotel map from the counter and tugged her bag along with her. No place to sit except at a bar, a slot machine, or a gaming table. Amy was supposed to have taken care of everything, but she guessed losing her voice had gotten in the way. *Slacker.* She laughed. That was totally untrue. Amy was awesome. Jesus, she was in a horrible mood. Maybe a drink *would* help. She walked to the closest bar and took the first free stool.

The bartender appeared quickly from around the corner of the horseshoe bar. "Can I get you something to drink?"

"A Corona, please." She fished her credit card out of her bag and set it on the bar.

"Lime and salt?"

"Yes. Please."

The bartender prepared the beer, set it in front of her, and took her card for payment. She came back shortly afterward. "This card was declined. Do you have another one?"

"What?" She found her phone in her bag and checked her banking app. "I have plenty of money in there."

"Sometimes they decline if you haven't let your bank know you're going out of town."

She shook her head. "This was a last-minute trip, and I completely forgot."

The bartender slid her drink to the closest video-poker machine. "Move over here, and I'll make it a comp."

"Thank you." She glanced at her name tag. "Morgan. I shouldn't be here long. Just waiting on my room." She blew out a breath of frustration as she slid to the next stool." I wasn't supposed to be here at all, but someone got sick, and now I have to fill in for her."

"Don't worry about it. Take your time and relax."

She opened her mobile-banking application again and created an online travel notification to let the bank know she was in Las Vegas and that she'd be returning home Monday. After a short minute she received a confirmation that she was able to use her debit card again.

She waved down the bartender and held up her card. "This should be good now."

"Great. You can use it on the next one."

"There won't be a next one tonight. As soon as my room is ready, I'm heading to bed."

"Well, tomorrow night, then." Morgan gave her a smile and continued making drinks for other customers.

. "Okay. Thanks." She slipped her card back into her bag. "Will you be working?" She'd at least drop by to give her a tip for being so nice. She squeezed the lime wedge, dropped it into her beer, raised it to her lips, and let the cool beer wash across her tongue. Flights always left her thirstier than normal.

"Should be. If I'm busy, Blair will take care of you." She pointed to the dark-haired bartender at the other side of the horseshoe bar.

Was that a brush-off? Even in Vegas she couldn't get an attractive woman to pay attention to her. The story of her life.

As she drank, she watched the game on the large TV suspended above the bar. The cold beer cooled her drier-than-usual throat. She hoped she wasn't coming down with strep too. Being sick in a hotel would be a disaster, especially with no one to take care of her. Not that she had anyone at home to do that, but at least she'd be in her own bed. She glanced at the date on her watch. She'd seen Amy yesterday, and she hadn't seemed sick, but she could've been running a low fever. Strep usually took two to five days to get her into bed for no good reason, so if she was exposed, she might make it through the weekend without showing symptoms if she did catch it. Maybe this would be her lucky weekend.

❖

Blair polished the highball glasses with a bar towel as she watched Morgan interact with a brunette who'd taken a seat at the bar. She'd seen the woman come out of registration and had expected her to head directly to the elevators, as most guests usually did. The bar was located strategically between the front door and the check-in area to catch tired, hot, thirsty guests when they first entered, generally not after check-in, though.

"What's going on with that one?" Blair motioned to the brunette. "You comped her drink, and she's not playing video poker."

"She's having a bad night."

"And you felt the need to cheer her up." She grinned. Morgan was always ready to please a lonely woman. "You get her room number yet?"

Morgan shook her head. "She's still waiting on her room." She glanced back to her. "She's not really my type." Morgan liked older women.

She stared at the woman for a minute. "Even mid-thirties is too young for you now?"

"Sometimes." Morgan chuckled. "That one's too stressed out right now. Not here because she wants to be."

"Oh?"

"She's filling in last minute for someone at a conference."

"Which one?"

"I didn't ask."

"Maybe she'll be more relaxed tomorrow night." She continued to watch the brunette as she drank her beer and kept her eyes glued to the TV.

"Probably won't be back."

"You never know." Blair took out her phone and searched for conferences in Las Vegas. The site she usually used came up, and she scrolled through the results. Only one conference in the hotel this weekend and it was for physical therapy. She glanced back at the woman. She wasn't large, nor was she small. Taller than most, with a bit of muscular definition in her arms peeking out just below the cap-sleeve, V-neck shirt. Physical therapy could be her profession.

She wandered toward her, checking other customers' drinks as she moved around the bar. "Can I get you another beer?"

"No, thanks. I'm about to fall asleep as it is." The woman rubbed her eyes. "This time-zone change is a killer."

"It can be." She was probably from the East Coast. "Make sure you order the continental breakfast for tomorrow, when you get to your room. The coffee-bar lines in the lobby are huge in the mornings."

"Thanks for the tip." The woman smiled, sipped her beer, and stared back at the TV.

Blair got busy making a drink for someone else at the other side of the bar, and by the time she looked back again, the woman was crossing the room toward the reception area. She paused for a moment to watch her. Distinct swagger and a lot of confidence in each step. Maybe being pulled into work tonight hadn't been so bad after all. She'd be keeping an eye out for that one during her usual shift tomorrow night.

CHAPTER FOUR

Rachel's presentation on managing pain through physical therapy had gone well. Every seat in the room had been full, and she'd spoken to at least a dozen people afterward who'd told her how much they enjoyed it. Several people whom she worked with through several different organizations located across the states had invited her to dinner, and though she'd tried to be polite and decline them all, somehow Suzanne, another physical therapist she'd known for years, had roped her in. She had to eat at some point, and Suzanne was easy to get along with, so she'd accepted. Catching up with her would be fun, but she hadn't expected the four others she'd invited along. Suzanne always did like to be surrounded by people.

They'd been seated quickly at this Italian restaurant, which she was thankful for. She was famished. Glancing around the table at the people she'd just met, she tried to fit a name with each face. It was no use. She'd already forgotten their names except for Suzanne. Thank God they were still wearing their conference badges. She would've taken hers off as soon as she left the area if she'd gone to her room instead of having dinner with everyone.

As she looked over the menu the waiter handed her, she wished she was back home getting ready for the First Friday art event. Her mouth watered as she thought of the vodka pasta at the little Italian restaurant next door to the gallery. Eating seemed to be the main point of her social life lately—the only time she got to interact with other people, to spend time with Shay. She glanced up from the menu. She was in good company tonight, surrounded by plenty of lovely women to converse with, but none of them sparked her libido even a tiny bit. Most of them were married anyway, and she was already in love with one of those.

The waiter was back taking orders around the table. New friend number one ordered rigatoni Bolognese, while number two ordered spaghetti carbonara. Number three was disappointed they didn't have lasagna and ordered pollo parmigiana instead. Suzanne ordered steak, which was surprising, since she'd chosen the Italian restaurant.

"And for you, miss?"

She was so hungry she could eat it all at this point. She glanced back at her menu. "I'll have the pappardelle pesce and a house specialty salad." It would be too much. All the restaurants in Vegas charged a lot, but they gave you plenty of food. If she couldn't be in the company she longed for, she would indulge in the food while she was here.

"I'm sorry Amy is sick, but I'm glad you were able to make it in her place." Suzanne smiled.

"Me too." She was sorry about the Amy-being-sick part but still not thrilled to be here. Now to get the spotlight off her. "How's everything going with you and your clinic?"

"It's good. We've finally expanded and brought in a few new therapists." Suzanne had recently partnered with another therapist and opened their own clinic within a popular gym in her area. "It's really surprising how many walk-ins we get now."

"I can imagine that being so available inside a gym has increased your business."

"Have you ever thought of doing something similar outside of the hospital?" This wasn't the first time Suzanne had asked Rachel that question.

"I have, but I like where I work. The hospital is dedicating more funding to the department, and we've expanded quite a bit over this past year."

"That's good news." Suzanne smiled. "If you ever want to discuss this subject more, just let me know. I'll be glad to share my business plan with you."

"Thanks. I appreciate that." It wasn't going to happen. Rachel liked having a stable job without worrying about where her paycheck was coming from.

The waiter's timing was perfect. He set a huge salad in front of Suzanne and then one in front of her. All attention was diverted to food now, with minimal conversation.

Rachel plowed through more salad than she should've, even after sharing with one of the other ladies. The house-made vinaigrette dressing was just tart enough to give the greens a wonderful kick.

Suzanne pushed her salad aside and glanced Rachel's way. "The woman at the registration desk told me there's a winery not far off the strip. I thought you and I could go tomorrow for a tour."

"Can I let you know in the morning? I might like to attend a couple of sessions." She was fibbing but thought she might do some shopping.

"Oh." Suzanne pulled her eyebrows together. "I was sure you'd want to go, so I've already bought the tickets." She handed her a brochure.

"Okay. Then I guess I will." She slipped the brochure into her bag but didn't particularly like Suzanne's assumption. However, she didn't want to hurt her feelings.

She was already full by the time her main course arrived, but she would make a gracious attempt to eat some of the dish so she wouldn't offend the chef. She spun a wad of pasta onto her fork and held back a moan as the deliciousness exploded in her mouth. None of this was going to waste.

After the plates had been cleared, and a cup of coffee and more conversation, she was ready to go—had been for the last thirty minutes while everyone talked shop. She had thoroughly enjoyed the pasta, but the entire meal had been too much, and her stomach was about to explode. The waitress finally delivered the check, and she tossed fifty dollars onto the tray. That should cover her dinner, drink, and leave a good tip. Several people at the table haggled over their part of the bill but eventually threw in what was needed to make the total.

She leaned into Suzanne, wrapped her arm around her shoulder, and gave her a quick hug. "I'm heading to my room."

"I'll meet you in the lobby tomorrow morning, say around seven?" Suzanne raised her eyebrows. "We can have breakfast before the wine tour."

"Yeah. Sure." She hadn't planned on breakfast either. Hadn't planned on the wine tour, but it seemed now she was stuck.

Suzanne smiled widely. "I'm really looking forward to it."

"Me too." She stood and slung her conference bag over her shoulder. "It was nice meeting you all." She gave the rest of the ladies a wave.

They all said their good-byes, and Rachel raced out of the restaurant. She didn't intend to spend the rest of evening with colleagues talking about work. She was done with all that and ready for a beer. A game had to be playing on TV she could watch somewhere. The bar where she was last night was a good place to start. It was in the hotel and close enough to the elevators to escape to her room when she'd had enough of all the people and noise.

After she found an empty seat at the end of the bar, she took several pamphlets from her bag. She glanced at the schedule and then set it aside to look at the winery-tour brochure. The woman at the conference registration desk had mentioned it and made it sound fabulous. She guessed that's why Suzanne couldn't refuse. She was an easy sell for conference activities. Apparently, a whole bunch of people had bought tickets. She'd overheard Suzanne talking about it to one of the other ladies at dinner—she'd probably convinced them all to go. Suzanne was going to have a lot of company on the tour. She set it aside and perused the rest of the paper, which advertised plenty of shows she could catch, but she hated going solo to those. If nothing else, she could go shopping like she'd originally planned. She picked everything up, shoved it into her bag, and slung the strap over her knee. Besides sleeping and possibly a little light gambling at the blackjack table, she hadn't really decided how to spend the rest of her weekend here.

"Nice to see you again, Rachel." The bartender smiled widely.

She pulled her eyebrows together "How did you know…" It hit her as the bartender glanced lower and pointed to her conference badge. She removed it from around her neck and tucked it away in her bag. Wasn't anonymity considered a perk in Vegas?

"Corona. Right?" Emerald-green eyes held her gaze.

"Yes. Please." The name was easy, but she also remembered her drink. She glanced at her name tag, which had been hidden behind her auburn hair last night, as she prepared the glass with lime and salt. She tilted the glass, poured the beer into it, and slid it in front of her. "Thank you, Blair."

"My pleasure." Blair smiled widely. "Just the one, or do you want to start a tab?"

"I'll probably have another. Stay and watch the game for a bit. Can I bill it to my room?"

"Absolutlely." She printed off the check and slid it in front of her to sign.

Rachel tried to be discreet but couldn't help but watch Blair's hips sway as she walked to the center of the bar with the charge slip. She was very attractive, dressed in black slacks and a form-fitting black polo shirt that clung tightly to her chest.

Rachel was sipping her beer as she watched the game when her phone lit up with an incoming FaceTime call. It was Shay. She immediately picked it up and answered.

"I miss you." Shay's lips twisted into a frown. A door closed behind her. It looked like she was walking out of the gallery.

She grinned. It was nice to be missed. "It can't be all that bad there without me. You've got food, wine, and lots of people to mingle with."

"I do have wine." Shay held up her glass. "But you know I hate mingling."

"Where's Chloe?" No one seemed to be with Shay.

"She's wrapped up inside with a new client." The picture skewed when Shay took a seat, and the gallery window appeared behind her.

Thank God she was stationary now. The camera movement was making Rachel dizzy. "So, you're sitting outside at one of the bistro tables drinking alone?"

"Yep." Shay nodded. "And I might be a little tipsy."

Rachel looked at her watch. It was just before seven o'clock here, so that would make it about ten there. A couple of hours into the event. "Do you have some food to go with that wine?"

"Not yet. My guardian angel is away in Las Vegas, so I'm drinking my dinner tonight." Shay took another sip of wine. "When are you coming back?"

"I'm here until Monday." Shay often didn't bother to eat at Chloe's events. Rachel always made sure she got fed on those occasions. More often than not they would miss the entire middle of the event and go to the restaurant next door to eat while Chloe mingled. She minimized the call and quickly typed a text to Chloe.

Shay needs food. Now.

A few minutes later a response came through. *How do you know? Aren't you out of town?*

She called me. She's out front at one of the tables drinking wine and looks a little glassy-eyed.

Chloe's next message came through quickly. *Thanks. I'll take care of it.*

Rachel expanded the call again. "It looks busy there tonight." She could see lots of people through the gallery window behind Shay.

"It is. Way too many people are inside. It's claustrophobic. How's the weather there?"

"Hot." She had no idea why anyone would come here in the middle of summer. It was only May, and the temps were in the nineties, the air super dry. It was ridiculous.

Shay's attention left the screen and she smiled. "Hey."

She heard Chloe's voice "I brought us some food to share."

"That's so sweet of you." Shay grinned as her gaze went sideways. Rachel's stomach tightened at her response to Chloe.

"Who are you talking to?" It seemed Chloe wasn't going to give it away that she'd contacted her.

"It's Rach. She's at a sports bar in Vegas."

The screen scrambled, and then Chloe appeared on the screen. "I've got her. Thanks for the heads-up." The phone went dark. Chloe seemed a bit annoyed, but whatever. She's *her* wife, and she should be watching out for her—paying more attention to her like she promised. That problem seemed to be arising between them again.

"Anytime," she said into the air with a growl as she dropped her phone to the bar.

She'd been making it easy for Chloe at her art events by keeping Shay occupied, an activity that probably wasn't good for herself. She hadn't quite been able to cut the tie with Shay since she'd been her physical therapist, and she honestly didn't know if she'd ever get past her feelings for Shay. She hadn't planned on having such a response—hadn't ever acted on or really embraced it, but she couldn't seem to let it go. It was unethical to become involved with a patient, but something drew her to Shay.

She'd tried to push the feelings out of her heart, or at least to a darkened corner, but it would take more than that to kill them. She'd have to stop seeing Shay, stop being her friend, and she didn't know if she could do that—didn't know if she wanted to.

If Shay and Chloe broke up again, could Shay be true to any woman other than Chloe? The continual question haunted her. The fact that Chloe had taken Shay back showed they were both in their marriage for the long haul. At least for now.

CHAPTER FIVE

B lair couldn't help but overhear Rachel's phone conversation. She'd been staying close and keeping an eye on her since she sat down. "Sounds like your girlfriend is missing you."

"Not my girlfriend. Just a friend."

"Doesn't sound like she knows that." From her observation of the conversation the woman seemed to have drunk-dialed her, which meant some sort of feelings were there.

"We're both clear on that fact. As is her wife." Rachel seemed to be scrutinizing her.

Blair raised her eyebrows. "Oh." She set another beer in front of her. "Sorry. I didn't mean to eavesdrop." She was correct. The girl on the phone was a touchy subject.

"You're fine. My friend was talking pretty loudly. She's a little tipsy."

"And you were supposed to be with her?"

"Yeah. Had to come to a conference instead. The trip was pretty last-minute." Rachel gripped the beer glass between her hands.

"I hope she makes it home okay." Prying information wasn't easy.

"She will. I let her wife know." Rachel took a gulp of beer and then laced her fingers together on the bar.

"Sounds like you're a pretty good friend." *Or something more.*

"I try." She took another drink before she focused on the TV.

"How long are you in town for?"

"Until Monday. Would've been out of here sooner, but I didn't make the flight reservations, and the cost to change them is ridiculous."

"I guess Vegas isn't your cup of tea."

"It's okay." Rachel shook her head. "I'm just not a big gambler."

That was good to hear. Not that Blair was invested in this one, but she was definitely attractive, seemed smart, and friendly enough. Their interaction was sure making her evening shift go by faster.

"Hey, Blair." Morgan called from the opposite side of the horseshoe bar. "Can I get some help for a minute?"

She picked up Rachel's beer and slid a new napkin under it. "I'll be right back."

"I'll be here." Rachel slipped her fingers around her glass and focused on the TV.

She turned and headed to the other side of the bar. "Who needs a drink?"

"I've got it." Morgan grinned.

"Then why did you call me over?"

Morgan glanced over her shoulder toward Rachel. "Seems like you and the lovely lady from last night are getting along."

"Just normal chitchat."

"Oh?" Morgan raised an eyebrow. "Seems like more than that."

"Not really."

"She looks a lot more relaxed than she was last night."

"Yeah. She is. She said she had to come to a conference last-minute." Blair wouldn't call Rachel relaxed. It seemed that the phone call had put her on edge.

"I bet you could make a night of it." Morgan raised her eyebrows. "Why don't you try one of your verses on her?"

"Nope. I'm done with that. All it did was bring me a woman who was in love with someone else." Even though she and Tess had become close friends, she'd still felt the rejection.

"But didn't making that happen give you all the good feels?"

"Yeah. Sure." It gave her the feels all right, but she wouldn't call them good. "Becoming another woman's matchmaker is overrated." Especially when she thought she'd be part of the match.

"So, you're just going to give up on love completely now?" Morgan opened a beer and set it in front of another customer, whose bottle was almost empty.

"Not completely, but it's on the back burner for now until I save enough money to start my business back in Florida."

"Maybe she'd be open to having a little bit of fun while she's here." Morgan nodded at another customer, who held up their empty glass, and began mixing another drink.

"You never know." She didn't mingle with customers often, but she'd been thinking the same thing.

"How about we make a little friendly wager, you and I?" Morgan tugged her lip to the side. "No money involved. Just a little fun with the out-of-towner."

"Absolutely not." She shook her head. "You're welcome to try, but I'm not betting on her."

"Challenge accepted." Morgan set the drink on the bar in front of the customer before she spun and sped around the bar.

Blair watched as Morgan turned on the charm, but Rachel didn't seem interested. She glanced at her once or twice and gave her a smile but focused mainly on the TV attached to the bar. Something about Morgan striking out gave Blair a bit of satisfaction.

Morgan came around to the other side again. "Good luck with that one. She's not interested in anything but the game she's watching." She glanced over her shoulder. "Must have money on it."

"Must have." From Rachel's comment about gambling before, she doubted it.

"I hope you're up to the challenge."

"There's no challenge—and no bet." Blair turned and went through the middle divider to the other side of the bar. By the time she got back to Rachel, she noticed that her beer was almost empty. "Can I get you another one?"

Rachel nodded as she glanced at Morgan. "What's her story?"

"You don't want to hop on that train. I promise you." She glanced over her shoulder at Morgan. "She's full of energy—never stops." She prepped a fresh glass with salt and lime before she popped the top off another beer and poured it into a glass, then slid it in front of Rachel.

"I can see that. She's very chatty." Rachel took a sip of her beer as she watched Morgan through the center of the bar. "I hope I didn't hurt her feelings."

"Nah. I'm sure she's fine." A little bruised ego, but Morgan would be okay. Her confidence rarely wavered, and she always moved on quickly.

❖

Rachel watched Blair as she interacted with customers at the bar. *She's hot, funny, and seems to be smart as well.* She noticed her rubbing her neck several times and was at it again when she came back to check her beer. "You seeing someone for that neck issue?"

Blair dropped her hand. "What makes you think I have a neck issue?"

"You've been rubbing it off and on all evening." She looked at her half-full beer, moved it slightly. "Plus, I'm a physical therapist. I can tell you're hurting."

"It's been bothering me for a while. This bar's too low." Blair gripped the edge with her fingers.

"I can help you with that." She waved her to the end of the bar as she got up from the stool.

Blair flipped the bar flap open and walked toward her.

"Turn around." Rachel massaged her shoulders and then her neck. She could feel Blair relax into her hands as she soothed the knots, and when she let out a soft moan, something stirred within Rachel. She slid her hands from Blair's neck and rubbed them together, trying to discharge the electricity from her system. "That should do you for a while." She took in a deep breath and went back to her seat. "I know a few exercises you can do to help as well."

"Oh, yeah?"

"I can show you." She stood. "Stand tall with your arms at your side, and place your right hand on your head with your fingers pointing to the left side." She performed the action and waited for Blair to do the same. "Now gently pull your head toward the right side until you feel a stretch in the left side of your neck." She watched Blair mimic her actions. "Hold it that way for twenty to thirty seconds before you return your head to the center."

"Wow. I can really feel that burn."

"Good." That meant it was working. "Your neck is pretty tense. Now do the same on the other side." Blair switched hands on her head and continued stretching her neck.

"That's astounding." Blair smiled widely as she dropped her hands to her side. "I guess this makes you my official physical therapist."

"For the night, anyway." She laughed. "I'm sure your back could use some relief as well. If I had you in my office, I'd give you a full massage."

Blair raised an eyebrow. "You would, would you?"

Rachel's cheeks heated. She hadn't meant that to sound the way it had, but she'd go with it. "You'd be amazed at the magic my fingers can work on your body."

"I'm sure I would be." Blair glanced at the other end of the bar, where someone was holding up their glass, and hesitated for a few seconds. "I'll be back in a bit."

Rachel was relieved to get a moment to regroup. This conversation was turning into more than she'd planned, and to be honest, she wasn't sure quite how far she wanted to take this interaction with Blair. She pulled her padfolio out of her bag and set it on the bar. Then she tried to expand on a few notes she'd written earlier to focus her mind differently. The distraction working the other end of the bar was too much to ignore. She checked to be sure the several business cards she'd collected were secured in one of the slots, adding her own to the top, before she closed the leather brief and ran her hand across the smooth cover. A short diversion from her life might be good for her. *After all, what happens in Vegas stays in Vegas, right?*

CHAPTER SIX

Even though it was way past her bedtime at home, Rachel was still full of energy. Blair had certainly kept her interested this evening. *She's probably friendly with all the customers at the bar.* She'd rolled the dice and decided to let loose—take a chance on getting more acquainted with Blair. She wasn't up for flat-out rejection, so she'd left her padfolio, hoping that Blair would return it. If she did, then she'd know Blair was interested. If Blair didn't bring it back, which it appeared she might not since she'd left the bar over an hour ago and was still alone, no harm done. She would swing by and pick it up in the morning.

She emptied her conference tote onto the bed and looked through the packet she'd received from the desk when she checked in. She plucked the wine-tasting tour information from it to review again. She had to be in the lobby by ten a.m. to make the shuttle that had been arranged to take them to the Las Vegas wine country. Suzanne had said breakfast was at seven, though. She'd probably told the same thing to everyone who was at dinner tonight, which was fine. Rachel really had nothing else to do. She could spend only so much time in the casinos and bars before she got bored.

The knock on the door startled her. She raced to it and looked through the peephole. A shiver ran through her when she saw Blair standing in the hallway. She stood back and took in a deep breath. She wasn't good at casual. She heard another soft knock. *Open the door, idiot. This is what you wanted.* She pulled it open.

"Hi." Blair cleared her throat. "You left your folder at the bar." She held it up.

"Oh, wow. I totally forgot about that."

"I figured you might need it for the rest of the conference."

"I will. Thanks." She had no plans to attend the rest of the conference. "Where are my manners? Come in, please." She pulled the door open wider and made room for Blair to pass, her energy off the charts.

"Okay. Sure." Blair walked a few feet inside and turned around. "Nice room."

"My friend booked it." She let the door close.

"The one you replaced?"

"Yeah." The conversation, the eye contact—everything became awkward. "Why are you here?" She wanted to clarify but didn't know how.

"I was returning your folder." Blair tilted her head. "Why did you invite me in?"

"I don't know. Maybe I shouldn't have." She hadn't expected to be so unsure—thought she could be cool about it. She'd had the occasional encounter, but it was usually with women she'd gotten to know better and spent more time with beforehand.

"You're nervous." Blair smiled softly.

"I guess I am. This isn't something I do—invite women I barely know into my room and—"

"Want to fuck them?" Apparently, Blair was taking the direct approach.

She tingled all over. "Yes. That." The attraction was undeniable.

"You're cute when you blush. Do you know that?" Blair moved closer. "Do you want me to leave?"

"No. Don't." She didn't know if she was attracted to Blair or to the anonymity of it all, but she wanted this.

"Okay. Then just relax." Blair reached forward, removed the hairband from Rachel's hair, and mussed it with her fingers. "You have lovely hair."

"It's kind of a mousy brown and needs to be cut." She grabbed a strand and twirled it around her finger.

"Shh." Blair brushed her lips lightly across her cheek, then whispered in her ear. "Stop talking yourself down. You're beautiful." She trailed her lips across her jaw to Rachel's lips. The kiss was soft and sweet. "Your mouth is perfect."

Rachel shivered as Blair's fingers swept slowly down her neck across her collarbone and followed the edge of her V-neck shirt. The next kiss was harder—longer. Blair using the tip of her tongue to trace the inside of Rachel's lips had her wanting more. Wanting it now. She hooked her hand behind Blair's neck and held firm as she took charge, pushing her tongue into Blair's mouth, seeking the slick softness inside. Blair pressed against her, reached around and grabbed her ass to gain more friction. Rachel tried to contain her excitement, but she hadn't been this wet in a long time—hadn't let anyone this close in a while—hadn't had someone want her like this in forever. If the foreplay was any indication, this was going to be a spectacular night.

"You're not drunk, are you?" Blair whispered as she moved her lips down her neck.

"You know how much I drank tonight." She threw her head back, giving more access.

"I only know what I served you." Blair continued across her collarbone. "You want to do this, right?"

"I'm well aware of what I want." She backed up and pulled her shirt over her head. "How about you?" She couldn't stop now even if she wanted to.

Blair's eyes widened as she assessed her. "No second thoughts here."

Heat flared within Rachel as she quickly slipped her fingers under the edge of Blair's shirt and tugged it up. Blair joined in to finish taking it off. Soon they were engaged in another heated kiss while they fumbled to unfasten each other's bra. She felt hers pop open first and scrambled to release the clasp of Blair's. Suddenly it sprang open, and she pushed it from Blair's shoulders and let it drop between them, letting her own fall along with it. She cupped Blair's breasts in her hands. A shiver ran through her when Blair let out a moan and tugged her closer—skin to skin. Blair's was on fire, a substantial change from the cool air in the room.

They tumbled onto the bed, and Blair immediately began working the button and zipper on Rachel's jeans. The cool air blasted her as Blair stood to yank them from her hips and remove her own. Blair quickly blanketed her again, returning the warmth. The kiss that came next was long, slow, and erotic, their tongues exploring this newfound pleasure together. Blair cupped her breast in her hand as she sucked a nipple into her mouth, letting it slip out before she sucked it back in again. Then her hand slid methodically down from her breast, tracing the bottom of her rib cage across her hip to her belly and under the band of her underwear. She jolted when Blair slipped her finger between her folds and slid it across her clit.

Blair moaned. "You're ready for me."

"I was ready when you walked through the door."

Blair grinned and kissed her hard as she moved her finger up and then down, then inside, pausing a moment to circle her clit with her thumb.

"Oh my God." She squirmed beneath her. "More of that. Right there." She placed her hand on top of Blair's, producing more pressure.

Blair followed her direction, and she tumbled into orgasm quickly, continuing the rhythm until she laced her fingers with Blair's to make her stop.

"Sorry. Was I too eager?" Blair situated herself into the crook of Rachel's arm.

"No. That was probably me. It's been a while since I've had an orgasm by another woman."

Blair lifted her head and leaned up on her elbow. "Why is that?"

"I don't socialize much." She took in a deep breath as contentment filled her. "I work a lot." That wasn't all true, but she wasn't ready to go into the details of her life with a stranger.

Blair rolled her lips in. "If you're wondering, I don't usually sleep with women I meet at the bar."

"Then why me?" Rachel was curious. There were plenty of women in Vegas.

"I don't know. You were nice, friendly, and killer gorgeous." Blair raised an eyebrow, and gave her a sexy grin.

"You're already in my bed, so you don't need to lie." She'd never thought of herself as more than adequate in the beauty department. She'd always had to work to gain a woman's interest.

Blair widened her eyes. "Oh my God. You really don't know how gorgeous you are, do you?" Blair let her gaze roam across Rachel down to her toes and back to her eyes.

The discomfort overwhelmed Rachel, and she grabbed the sheet with one hand to pull it over them.

"Don't." Blair stopped her. "I'm planning to travel across this wonderful oasis plenty more times tonight, and I want to see where I'm going."

Her cheeks heated. "That performance deserves something in return." The kiss that came next was just as passionate as their first, and when Blair slipped her fingers between her folds again, she was ready to start all over. Blair seemed to like giving, so Rachel wouldn't battle her for control. She'd let Blair take her again—let herself be transported to places she hadn't been in a long time.

CHAPTER SEVEN

B lair polished glasses for the wine flights as she stood behind the tasting bar at the winery. Staying in bed this morning had been much more tempting than her second job there.

If only Rachel had felt the same. She couldn't wipe last night from her mind if she wanted to. The whole experience had been wildly intense. It was as though they'd craved each other—had been kept apart for thousands of years only to rediscover an intimacy they'd been destined to find. She'd been disappointed when she'd awoken to an empty room this morning, with only a note on the bedside table. She took it from her pocket and read it again.

Blair,
Had to leave early for a conference commitment. You were sleeping so peacefully, I didn't want to wake you. Order room service if you like. You've made a horrible trip more wonderful than I could have ever imagined.
Rach

Rachel had left her alone in her room. Her suitcase and all her belongings were still there, so she was coming back, but she hadn't indicated that she wanted to see her again. She didn't know what to do. Should she just leave it as a wonderful night with a gorgeous woman, or should she show up at her door again this evening? Yet that might be too presumptuous—and awkward—if Rachel didn't plan to see her again or wasn't alone. She shoved the note into her pocket and headed to the tasting bar. She would focus on work for now. The first tour bus had just arrived.

She watched the people filter inside. Her stomach bounced. Rachel was trailing along at the end of the crowd, lagging behind, texting on her phone. She was just as gorgeous today as she had been last night, despite her lack of sleep. After Rachel's early exit this morning, Blair had only half expected to see her again. But now that she was here, she couldn't avoid her. Didn't want to.

"Hey, Morgan. I'm gonna give someone a personal tour. Can you cover for me?" This request was going to fire off a string of questions.

Morgan glanced over her shoulder at Rachel. "I see you won the bet." Unfortunately, Morgan had connected the dots.

"There is *no* bet." She refused to fill Morgan in on the particulars of last night, but she couldn't deny it either.

"Right. You need me to cover for you at the bar tonight?"

"No." She shook her head. "I'm off until Tuesday." She'd traded shifts with someone Thursday night…the night she'd first seen Rachel. Lady Luck seemed to be on her side this weekend.

Morgan glanced over her shoulder. "I'll find someplace else to stay, just in case."

"Thanks. I owe you."

"You bet you do." Morgan winked before she pushed her toward Rachel. "Go. Relax. Have some fun for once."

She located Rachel across the room, studying the maps on the wall of various wine grape locations that included maps of Spain, Italy, and France.

"Can I offer you a personal tour of the winery?" They were allowed to give personal tours. Did it really matter if the customer hadn't requested one?

Rachel turned and smiled widely. "I would love that." Rachel seemed surprised to see her and not uncomfortable at all—happy even. "You work here too?"

"I do." She worked wherever she could right now.

"I wasn't aware." Rachel grinned and lowered her voice. "Should I apologize for keeping you up all night?"

"Never apologize for something so sweet as that." Blair shook her head. "I'm just sorry I wasn't up to give you a proper send-off this morning." She waved her hand in front of her. "This way to the barrels, miss." She led Rachel through the tasting room to the door that connected to the warehouse area. "It's not much, but it gets the job done."

Rachel assessed the stacks of barrels. "How many types of wine do they make?"

"Currently only five." She moved closer to the barrels and pointed to the names stamped on the ends. "This one is a 2021 burgundy."

"How long does the wine stay in the barrels?"

"It depends on the type of grape and the vintner, but red wines usually one to two years. White wines are less than that." She led Rachel to the area of the room where they tested the wine.

Rachel picked up a wine beaker and stared at the lines on the glass, then set it down on the metal lab table before she studied the equipment. "I didn't realize winemaking was so complicated." She raised her hand. "Beer drinker, here."

"There's definitely science behind the wine."

"I would've never thought all this would be located in such an industrial area."

"It's not rustic and old-school like you might see in Napa Valley, but the wine is outstanding. They have all kinds of activities scheduled during the week. If you're here, you should try wine yoga. It's a whole different experience."

"All kinds of images are popping into my head."

"As they should." She grinned. "Exercise and wine midafternoon make for a helluva happy hour."

"I'll have to see if I can find a class when I get home."

"And home is?" She shouldn't ask but really wanted to know.

"Too far to join here, I'm afraid."

Seemed Rachel wasn't going to divulge any personal information. This was just a weekend dalliance. She was okay with that, hadn't planned on anything more, but was a little surprised at her disappointment. "Ready to head back?" They didn't have much conversation as they strolled to the tasting room. It was a short walk but seemed like miles of awkward steps. "I know you said you prefer beer, but do you want to taste some of the wine?" She raised her eyebrows. "We have several varieties on the menu today. Riesling,

Zinfandel, Syrah, and a dry white made from grapes primarily sourced from the nearby Amargosa Valley. There's also hard cider on tap. One of the vineyards where the grapes are grown isn't far, if you'd like to see it."

"You're just full of knowledge." Rachel grinned. "Seeing the vineyard would be awesome. I was hoping to visit some of the less touristy sights while I'm here." She glanced at the wall poster of how to choose the right wine. "Are you working all day? Maybe you could show me around." A blush covered Rachel's cheeks. "I'm sorry. That was pretty presumptuous."

"Not at all." She raised her eyebrows and held back a grin. Her weekend was looking up after all. "I'm scheduled until four but might be able to break free earlier." She was scheduled all day, but she would get Morgan to cover for her. She wanted to spend more time with Rachel.

Rachel waited in front of the entrance while Blair arranged to leave early. She hoped there wouldn't be any repercussions. She'd hate for Blair to get into trouble for spending time with her. When she'd woken this morning, Blair was out cold. Not even a good shake could wake her—probably a good thing or Blair would've pulled her back into bed for another round. She would've missed her breakfast date with Suzanne and then the winery excursion. Spending all day in bed with Blair would've been a tempting distraction. Now that she'd been placed in the same proximity as Blair this afternoon, for whatever reason, it seemed like fate had thrown them together again.

Blair rushed through the door. "All set." She made a move to reach for Rachel's hand but waved her toward the parking lot instead. "My car's right over here." Blair led her to a royal-blue Mustang convertible.

"I have a convertible too." Rachel contemplated opening Blair's door for her but didn't want to make her uncomfortable. Instead, she went to the passenger side and got in.

Blair slid into the driver's seat. "What kind?"

"Camaro."

"Those are nice. A little out of my price range, though." Blair pulled her door shut.

"Do you put the top down much here? I would think it would be too hot."

Blair fired the engine. "It's way too hot during the day. I drop it only in the evenings, after the sun has already gone down." She glanced behind her as she backed out of the parking space. "Do you mind if we stop by my place so I can change?" Blair glanced at her and raised her eyebrows briefly as she returned her attention to the front. "It's not too far from here."

"Not at all." Rachel focused on the windshield, wondering if going to Blair's house would interrupt their plans for the vineyard.

As they pulled into the subdivision where Blair's house was located, Rachel was surprised. It wasn't at all what she'd expected. The exteriors of the houses in the neighborhood boasted stucco walls and beautifully tiled roofs. "Wow. Your house is gorgeous." The Spanish-style home had a tower, and if that wasn't romantic enough, it also had wrought-iron balconies. She could live in a place like this.

Blair found her key to unlock the door. "I'm not a big fan of stucco, but it maintains a cooler temperature inside during the warmer months."

Rachel touched the rough external wall. "Really? I love it." Something about the warm comfort that came with a Spanish flair appealed to her.

She followed Blair through the door and found the inside just as inviting. Massive beams spanned the ceiling, and heavy doors added more warmth and interesting architectural details. A common area seemed to be the nucleus of the home, with the rest designed around it.

"I'll be right back." Blair trailed off down the hallway to one of the rooms. The master bedroom, Rachel assumed.

She walked over to the span of plate-glass windows across the living area and looked out onto the spacious courtyard. The whole place was warm and inviting. How could Blair afford such a large house on a bartender's salary?

"Ready?" Blair appeared beside her.

"Yep." She didn't veer her gaze from the courtyard. "Your place is really lovely."

"I'm glad you like it." Blair turned and headed to the door, opened it, and waited for her to exit.

Rachel slid into the passenger seat of the Mustang and buckled up. "Thank you for this. I honestly wasn't expecting to have my own private tour guide today."

"I bet I'm more entertaining than the driver who took you to the winery."

"As a matter of fact, the driver entertained us during the forty-five-minute experience by describing sites and Las Vegas history humorously."

"Challenge accepted." Blair smiled at her as she put the car into gear and backed out of the driveway.

"How is your neck is feeling?" She hadn't seen Blair rub it once today.

"Much better. Thanks to you. I'm going to recommend you to all my friends."

She laughed. "Get them lined up. I'm only here until Monday." Her phone rang, and she glanced at the screen, seeing that it was Chloe. "Sorry. I need to get this."

"No worries." Blair pulled into the convenience store on the corner down the street from the entrance to the subdivision.

Rachel hit the green button and held the phone to her ear. "Hello."

"Hey. I just called to apologize for cutting you off last night. Shay was drunk, just as you said, and I had to get her home."

Blair's hand landed on her shoulder. "Do you want something to drink?"

"Water," she said softly.

"Who's that?" Chloe asked.

Rachel glanced over her shoulder and glimpsed Blair heading into the convenience store. "A friend." A smoking-hot friend. She'd changed into blue skinny jeans and a light-blue, V-neck shirt.

Chloe's voice lightened. "Well, I'm glad you found someone to hang out with while you're there."

She was sure Chloe was happy for more reasons than one. "Me too. I was kind of dreading this trip, but it's turned out to be pretty nice."

"Awesome. You'll have to fill Shay and me in on your friend when you get back."

"Sure." She would do that but had no plans to tell them all the details of last night. She spotted Blair coming out of the store. "Hey. I have to go. I'll talk to you when I get home." She hit the end button before Chloe could respond.

Blair handed her a bottle of water as she got back into the car and screwed the top off her own, then took a drink before she dropped it into the center console. "It should take about thirty minutes to reach the vineyard from here."

The drive wasn't far, just as Blair had said. It was amazing how everything in Las Vegas seemed to be within an hour's car ride. Once parked, they headed directly to the field of grapevines. Blair led her down a row of them, pointing out the small bunches of grapes as they walked. The dialogue lessened, and she worried that Blair was tired of her. It was new to her that someone other than Shay was occupying her thoughts. She hadn't even glanced at her phone in the last hour to see if Shay had messaged. She was standing close to the grapevine, and suddenly Blair came closer. Was she going to kiss her?

Blair reached forward and took a leaf out of Rachel's hair and then tucked a strand behind her ear. "You had a souvenir hanging out up there." She grinned as she slipped her hand into hers and laced their fingers together.

Rachel's body lit up like fireworks on the Fourth of July. How could such a simple gesture send a simmering jolt through her so easily?

"Where do you want to go next?"

"You tell me. You're the native here." She was assuming but really didn't need to know otherwise if that wasn't the case.

"There's an old doll museum nearby, if you're into those kinds of antiques."

"Not so much."

"Are you sure?" Blair grinned as she raised her eyebrows. "They have real hair and teeth."

"Definitely no."

"Springs Preserve is close. We can do that next unless you want to trek out to the Valley of Fire in the Mojave Desert, which is about forty-five minutes away."

"Which one do you like best?"

"I like them both. The sandstone formations in the Valley of Fire are distinctively vibrant, and you can see plenty of rock art there, but with the temperature rising like it is, the preserve is probably better this time of day. They have the most beautiful botanical garden, plus some archeological sites."

Forty-five minutes of conversation in the car with Blair might be too much for her. "Let's do the botanical garden." She knew a little bit about plants native to Florida. It would be nice to find some desert plants that might possibly grow along with them in her garden.

"I don't know a lot about the plants here, but I have a friend who's been teaching me." Blair shook her head. "That's not completely true. She quizzes me incessantly, so I've been trying to learn more."

"That doesn't sound nice." How close was she with this friend? Did Blair sleep with many women? For all she knew, she could be one in a string of them.

"She's actually a close friend of my mom's—more like an aunt. That's the reason for the quizzing. She lives down the street from me, and we walk together sometimes in the early morning."

Why was she so relieved to hear that explanation? What business was it of hers if Blair slept with other women? "Not too early, I suspect, with your working hours at the bar."

"My schedule rotates. Sometimes I work days."

"What shift are you on tomorrow?" Probably shouldn't have asked that question.

"I usually have Sundays off." Blair gave her a sideways glance. "Lucky for you."

There it was again—that jolt to her midsection. "Yes. Lucky for me." The possibility of another night in bed with Blair excited her more than she'd expected.

"You want to grab something to eat? There's an In-N-Out Burger on the way."

"Fries animal style?"

"No other way."

"My mouth is already watering." She hadn't had one since the last time she was in Vegas. She couldn't pass up such a treat.

CHAPTER EIGHT

It wasn't too long after they'd eaten before they pulled up to the Mission-style building at the entrance of Springs Preserves. Rachel was stuffed from the burger and fries she'd practically inhaled. "There's a whole lot more to see here besides the botanical garden, if you're interested. Boomtown Village and the museum, just to name a couple. You could spend a full day here easily."

"Let's stick with the gardens for now, okay?" She wasn't up for a whole day of learning.

"That works for me." Blair headed toward the ticket counter.

"Let me get the tickets." Rachel reached into her bag and took out her wallet.

Blair held up her hand. "Nope. I got it. You're the visitor."

She wouldn't argue, but this didn't feel right. Blair hadn't planned on taking a random stranger she'd just met on a sightseeing trip today. Although last night had admittedly been mutually gratifying, she shouldn't have to absorb the cost of the tickets for today's excursion.

Blair returned with their tickets. "All set." She led her to the entrance to the botanical gardens.

"Wow. This is awesome. It's wild to see so much foliage in the desert."

"I know. I come here a lot just for the peace and quiet. It's very relaxing." Blair pointed toward one of the pathways. "The aloe area is huge, with oodles of types."

"Oodles?" She raised her eyebrows.

Blair smiled sheepishly. "What term would you use?"

"Many, lots, gazillions." She grinned. "But I like oodles best."

"Well, you'll see a gazillion pollinators down this trail." Blair took her hand and led her to an offshoot of the main trail. She stopped at a tall, orange-colored, blooming plant and studied it. "This is lion's tail. It attracts hummingbirds." Blair touched the swirling bloom and then moved on to the next. "This one's margarita something or other. I can't remember the whole name." Then she pointed to the purple and green ground cover next. "Alyssum here."

"And verbena." Rachel knelt to take in the scent. "I love the smell of this one."

Blair knelt next to her and did the same, then gazed into her eyes. They seemed to be having a moment. "You're beautiful when you smile."

"Sweet-talker." Rachel bolted up, shook the tingle away, and moved to the next section. "Is that grass over there?" She pointed to the green blanket of turf.

"Nope. Not much grass grows around here. It requires too much water. That's called dwarf carpet of stars."

Rachel knelt and ran her hand across it, let it tickle her palm. "Wow. This is so much softer than grass."

"Right? It looks just like grass, yet you don't have to water it but maybe a couple of times during the summer. It's a succulent native to South Africa. It never gets any taller than an inch or two and never needs to be mowed."

Blair sat and then sprawled across it on her back. "Come on. Try it." She patted the spot next to her.

Rachel lay next to her on the carpet of green and stared at the clear, blue sky.

Blair shifted on her side to face her. "Let me take you to dinner later, show you some sights after hours." Blair raised her eyebrows just a touch.

"I don't know. I'm scheduled to go on the Big Bus Open Top Tour tonight. Can you beat what's on that agenda?" Rachel bit her lip as she smiled. She'd signed up for the tour only to keep herself out of the bar, to prevent herself from running into the very person she was with right now.

"I might be able to provide a little more entertainment." Blair moved closer and gave her a scorching kiss, then caressed her back with her hand. Rachel enjoyed the thrill that shot through her before taking a deep breath to steady herself. "I think so too." Considering last night, she knew so. Blair was a whole lot of dynamite wrapped in a smoking-hot package. She only hoped she could keep this weekend in Vegas from exploding into her life in Florida. She wasn't ready for something that burned so hot on a regular basis.

"Come on." Blair shot up and offered her a hand. "Wanna go see the Seven Magic Mountains?" She led her to the car.

"What are they? I've been here a couple of times and never heard of those."

"They're fairly new compared to some of the sights, and at first, all the locals were like, what the heck are these random painted boulders and where did they come from? Because they seriously just showed up one day near Jean Dry Lake."

"Sounds weird."

"Totally. Seven towers of wildly colored rocks painted by some Swiss artist. I can honestly say they're pretty impressive when you see them up close, but they're kind of out of the way, and it might not be worth the drive to see them. "We can go if you want, though. It's a great photo-op place." They got in, and she fired the engine.

"Now I'm intrigued and have to see them."

"Okay." Blair grinned. "Then see them, we will." She pulled on to the interstate. "I'm not big on viewing large animals caged, but we can stop at Lion Habitat Ranch if you'd like."

"I'm with you there. I don't like that either."

"Speedvegas is that way if you want an adrenaline rush." She pointed to the exit sign. "It'll probably be busy, but I thought you might like it, since you drive a Camaro and all."

"No. I'm good with driving normal speeds." She'd had too many patients recovering from auto accidents to take random chances with her own life.

"There's also an ATV adventure on the way."

Another bone-breaking activity she could do without. "I'll stick with the crazy rocks. If that's okay."

"Definitely. I'm just the guide." Blair pulled her lips into a cockeyed smile.

They stayed on the highway as they drove ten miles south of Las Vegas until the rocks came into view, growing larger as they neared.

"Wow. These have to be more than thirty feet tall." She got out of the car and wandered closer to the brightly colored stones.

"Probably taller." Blair stared up into the air like a kid at an air show. "They were supposed to be here for only a couple of years, but people love them, so I guess they're gonna stay."

Her stomach grumbled.

"Hungry again?"

"Aren't you?" They'd spent more time at the botanical gardens than she'd thought. It had been hours since they'd eaten, the sun now starting to move to the west.

Blair took her hand and pulled her back to the car. "Just one more stop before dinner."

❖

Blair drove north from the Seven Magic Mountains past the Las Vegas Strip on I-15, then pulled into the parking lot of the Neon Boneyard Museum Park. She'd saved the best for last. It had tacked on an additional thirty minutes to their travels, but the experience would be worth the extra time. It was a spectacular sight any time of day, but just after dusk was the perfect opportunity to view the signs as they began to light. The sky was just dark enough to allow you to experience the neon colors and also see the entire signs as they appeared during the day.

"Ooh. I was hoping to see this while I was here. I've been to Vegas a few times and have never had time."

Rachel's giddy reaction made Blair's stomach swirl. "But you weren't going to mention it?"

"I figured if we didn't make it here today, I'd check it out tomorrow." Rachel glanced out the window. "Can we have dinner here?"

"The museum doesn't have much in the way of food. I don't recommend walking around this area in the evening. It's pretty sketchy. We would need to park and then get a Lyft or Uber to reach any restaurants from here." She found a spot in the lot, and they headed into the park. It was presumptuous of her, but she'd purchased the tickets online when she'd gone inside to change earlier today. Figured if things didn't work out today with Rachel, she'd come herself and eat the price of the additional ticket.

"Are we going on the tour?"

"We can if you want, but I've been here a few times and can probably give you just as much history about the signs without the crowd."

"Sounds good." Rachel followed her. "How long has this been here?"

"It was founded in 1996." They saw the usual palm trees, and the wide pathways were lined with large rocks, making the whole experience ever so rustically Las Vegas. She'd forgotten about the music playing in the background, which was so loud she could barely hear Rachel. Whispering in each other's ears was delightful, though.

Rachel stopped to look at the Barbary Coast signage, which featured a Tiffany-style glass and a burgundy and gold color scheme. "There's so much nostalgia here." The awestruck look in Rachel's eyes reminded Blair of a child seeing Christmas lights for the first time.

Blair couldn't help but stare—study the slope of her nose, the small cleft in her chin, the tiny lines around her blue eyes. Rachel was dazzling in the neon light—she was stunning in any light. How had she fallen into meeting this perfect woman?

Rachel cleared her throat, and Blair moved to the next sign. She'd caught her staring. "Did you know Elvis performed in Las Vegas for the first time at the Frontier in 1956?"

"I had no idea."

"And then there's Tim Burton's Lost Vegas exhibit. It's a larger-than-life collection of obscure signs, props, and memorabilia of pop culture. Not so nostalgic now, and no longer open. It was fabulous just the same."

"That's disappointing."

"I can show you a tour on social media later."

"I'd love to see it."

A couple and their wedding party were taking pictures in front of the Fishtail Arrow neon wedding sign. "Apropos, but not the most photogenic place here."

"Oh? Which sign would you use for your wedding pictures?"

"They provide a different site for elopements and weddings, which is awesome, but my favorite is down here." Blair slipped her hand into Rachel's and led her farther down the path. "The tall section of the Stardust sign."

"I can see why. It's magnificent." She took in the star-shaped pieces thrusting far into the air and the vibrant pastel colors. "I thought the Moulin Rouge would be perfect, but this one's much better. I'd probably choose the same."

Blair smiled like she'd just received the best compliment ever. "The Moulin Rouge is a good choice as well. It opened in 1955. Betty Willis, who created the Welcome to Fabulous Las Vegas sign, designed it too."

"You're just a fountain of knowledge. I'm impressed by your ability to remember the quirky details of vintage Vegas. Most people don't know any of that."

"It comes from a lot of bartender conversation. Gotta sell the city." They walked around someone with a camera pointed at the Stardust sign. "Pictures don't do that sign justice."

While she was whispering in Rachel's ear, Rachel turned her head quickly and kissed her right as the Hard Rock sign was lighting up. Blair felt as though she was lighting up as well. The lights pulsed up the neck of the guitar, and she could literally feel the energy coursing through her in the same rhythm. She tried to calm her reaction, but it was no use. Rachel flipped every one of her switches.

"That was nice." It was nicer than nice. It was spectacular.

Rachel pulled her lip up to one side. "I've been wanting to do that since you kissed me earlier, and something about this place..." She glanced at the signs. "Made it even more magical."

"Yes. It did." She squeezed Rachel's hand, and they moved along the pathway. "The Desert Inn operated from April 24, 1950 to August 28, 2000. It was the fifth resort to open on the Strip." Blair tugged her toward an area that was roped off.

"Wait. Isn't this off-limits?" Rachel scrunched her eyebrows.

She shook her head. "Not for us. I know a guy."

Rachel rushed farther down the pathway. "Is that the original Aladdin's lamp?"

"Yep. I think it was created about 1966. It used to be in the Fremont Street Experience exhibit, but they pulled it into the Boulevard Lot here in 2013."

"You think?" Rachel smiled as she raised her eyebrows. "Are we entering the sketchy-knowledge area?"

"Well, some of these are pretty unique and old, so yes."

"It's nice to know you're not afraid to admit you don't know something." Rachel stopped walking and kissed her again.

When the kiss ended, Blair took a breath to settle herself. "Oh. Well, I don't know a lot of things." She wrapped her arms around Rachel and kissed her deeply. Every part of her came alive—nerves sparking in a rhythmic pattern just like the signs surrounding them.

Blair tried to find her balance as she stumbled backward on one of the pathway rocks into one of the signs and then to the ground, pulling Rachel down with her. She wasn't done with this kiss yet. Something about doing it right out in the open made it all the more exciting. She let her hands explore Rachel's back and then her ass, pulling her hard against her.

She heard a cough, and then a deep male voice startled her out of her bliss. "You two need to take that outside the park."

"Oh my God." Rachel bolted upright and wiped the dust from her pants. "Apparently you don't know all the guys here."

"Apparently not." She shot up, grabbed Rachel's hand, and pulled her down the pathway and out of the park.

When they finally reached the parking lot and jumped into the car, they looked at each other and laughed.

Rachel scrunched down in her seat and peeked over the dashboard. "I haven't been caught making out since I was a teenager in the girls' bathroom at school."

"Same." It was well worth the embarrassment. She was still tingling. "The first time was behind the gym. The second in the school parking lot."

"Girl?"

"Absolutely." It was time to get somewhere they could be alone. "You want to have some dinner? I know a place with fabulous food in Chinatown." Narrowing the option would tell her if Rachel had the same thought.

"Chinese sounds great. It's my favorite."

She grinned. Blair's food of choice as well. "We can order takeout on the way back to my place."

"Oh. Okay." Rachel seemed hesitant. Maybe Blair had read the situation wrong.

"Don't worry. I'll have you back to the hotel before my car turns into a pumpkin." She lied. The way this night was going, she would never get Rachel back to her hotel until morning unless she insisted.

CHAPTER NINE

When they reached Blair's house, they sped into the bedroom and left the Chinese food on the table. They'd stopped halfway there for another scorching kiss, the energy between them was unreal. Their fifteen minute make-out session in the car in front of the restaurant while they waited for their food had been ridiculously hot. Blair's appetite for the food they'd ordered had totally disappeared.

Once they made it to the bedroom, Rachel's lips were on hers, her tongue doing magical things inside Blair's mouth, creating incredibly erotic sensations in the rest of her. She sat on the bed and tugged Rachel to her—onto her. Rachel straddled her as she unbuttoned her shirt, then let it drop from her shoulders before she quickly unclasped her bra. Blair couldn't help but stare at the glorious breasts as Rachel's bra slid down her arms. How had she found such a wizard who seemed to satisfy her every need? Rachel stood to unfasten her jeans, and Blair took over, then helped her push them to the floor, taking her panties with them.

"I need you naked."

Blair pulled her shirt over her head and tossed it to the floor before she popped the clasp of her bra and threw it in the same direction. She made quick work of the button on her pants. The zipper shot open when Rachel began pulling the pants from her hips.

Rachel's hand went quickly back to her hips. "I love these curves."

"Oh, yeah?" Blair crawled backward toward the headboard. "Show me how much."

A jolt of electricity shot through Blair when Rachel kissed her way up her thigh to her hip. The heat of her breath spiked the electricity higher as Rachel's lips touched her lightly. She jumped when Rachel's tongue trailed across the sensitive spot in the crease.

Rachel moaned as she slid a finger between Blair's folds. "You are so ready."

"You do that to me." Rachel twirled her thumb around her clit for a minute, and soon Rachel was buried between her legs with her tongue deep inside her. She began to quiver, let out a cry, and Rachel continued her pace as the orgasm ripped through Blair.

Rachel chuckled as she teased her with her tongue, watching Blair's stomach bounce with each stroke. Then her stomach growled loudly.

Blair laughed "Hungry?" They still hadn't eaten anything since the burgers they'd grabbed earlier.

"Famished." Rachel slipped out of bed. "The Chinese food is still on the table. Let's go get some and watch something on TV while we eat." Rachel found a robe that had been slung across a chair and slipped it on. "I'm stealing this."

"But I have plans for you." Blair patted the bed with her hand.

"Food first. As I recall, your couch looks pretty versatile." Rachel glanced over her shoulder and winked.

"We shall see." Blair pulled a T-shirt over her head and followed Rachel into the kitchen. A girl after her own heart. Blair had never been one to sit at the table and eat. The couch and coffee table were more her style.

"Bowls or plates?"

"Neither. Just give me a big fork, and I'm good with eating from the containers." Rachel scrunched her eyebrows. "Unless you're not."

"That works for me. Why dirty a dish if we don't have to?" She reached into the refrigerator for a couple of drinks. "Soda or water?"

"Water, please."

She grabbed two waters and carried them to the coffee table, along with forks and napkins.

"We clearly ordered too much." Rachel took all the containers out of the bag.

"Too bad you won't be here tomorrow for more."

That thought made her sad. It was weird how comfortable she was with this whole scenario. She hadn't invited anyone back to her place since she'd moved to Las Vegas. Hadn't wanted to at all. Maybe it was the fact that she might never see Rachel again, and she didn't know how to let her go.

She stared at Rachel for a moment as she ate. Rachel's dark hair flowed across her shoulders and into the hood of the fleece robe.

Rachel turned her head. "What?"

"My robe looks much better on you than it does on me." The neutral white made her crystal-blue eyes pop. Absolutely mesmerizing.

"It's so comfy." Rachel nuzzled her neck with the collar.

"It fits you perfectly."

They watched TV and passed the food between them, eating out of each other's on occasion. They hadn't been tense or anxious during their time together. It all felt natural. Blair could get used to this.

Rachel woke to Blair splayed across her, one arm around her waist, a leg entangled with her own. Blair had shown her so many new sights yesterday, not the least of which was her sweet, sexy body. They moved together really well, so well that Rachel would be perfectly content spending the rest of her time in Las Vegas wrapped up right here in bed with Blair. She didn't know which she'd enjoyed more last evening—the electric signs in the Neon Boneyard or the look in Blair's eyes as she described them to her.

She checked the time on her phone. It was still early in Las Vegas, but her internal clock was still set to Florida time. She saw several missed calls and texts from Shay. She'd been so immersed in Blair she hadn't even thought about Shay. That hadn't happened since she met Shay. She scrolled through the texts.

How's the conference going?

Are you okay?

You're not answering your phone.

She set her phone on the nightstand, but then the guilt set in. She had to at least let Shay know she was all right. She grabbed the phone and typed in a message. *Everything is fine. The conference is good.*

Shay wrote back immediately. *I was getting ready to call hotel security.*

Sorry. I'm kind of tired. She glanced at Blair still snuggled into her side. *The conference is keeping me occupied.* Not a total lie. Her night had been thoroughly exhausting.

I hope you're learning lots of new things.

She absolutely was doing that. *I am. Gotta go. Need to get ready for the day.*

Another message from Shay came back quickly. *Have fun. Can't wait to see you when you get back.*

Same.

She dropped her phone on the nightstand and nudged Blair, but she didn't budge. She had to go pee. As she began slipping from beneath her, Blair shifted and rolled to her back. She snuck out of bed and into the bathroom. It was small, just like the rest of the house, but not overly crowded with stuff and nicely decorated with hues of pastel purple and blue. She pulled on the robe that was hanging on the back of the door, unsure how it had ended up there last night, and made her way down the hallway. She glanced at the front door as she passed it. Freedom was within her grasp, but she didn't want to leave yet.

The kitchen was modern and looked like it had been remodeled recently. Did Blair own the place? As she recalled from the night before, it was lovely but looked small from the outside, yet inside it was much more spacious than she'd imagined. She opened a few cabinets and found a bag of coffee. It was a common coffeemaker, so she proceeded to make a pot. Coffee would be her only savior today.

After starting the brewer, she stretched and walked into the living room. A pleasant ache resonated in her shoulders. She wasn't quite as flexible as she used to be. She opened the multiple blinds to the backyard. No grass like home, just desert trees and bushes. The landscaping was perfect just the same, only different. How did people handle living in such extreme heat? If she merely walked outside, she broke into a sweat. The heat in Florida could be suffocating enough. At least this was dry heat, if that even made a difference.

When the coffee was ready, she poured herself a cup, sat on the couch, and clicked on the TV. It was a smart TV, so she settled on one of the streaming services—curious when she found another user on the list named Morgan. Was that the same Morgan from the bar? She clicked on Blair's favorites, which were full of crime shows, documentaries, action-hero films, and a few romantic comedies. A weird combination that oddly matched her own favorites.

❖

Blair woke up to an empty bed. When had Rachel slipped out of her arms? She sat up and caught the aroma of fresh coffee. Heading into the bathroom to go, she smiled when she realized her robe was missing from the hook on the door where she'd placed it last night. Apparently, Rachel had taken a liking to it. She went back into the bedroom and slipped on an oversized T-shirt before she went down the hallway to the kitchen.

The coffee was ready, an empty cup waiting on the counter for her. She filled it to the brim, took a sip, and refilled it. After their marathon night, she needed copious amounts of coffee. It was her energy elixir.

Rachel's voice floated from the living room. "Good morning."

She rounded the breakfast bar that separated the two rooms. "Why are you up so early?"

"It's not early on the East Coast."

A tidbit of information Rachel hadn't given her before. Rachel's fatigue the first night they'd met made sense now. "That internal clock can be a pain in the ass."

"Definitely." Rachel was scrolling through her favorites list on her streaming service. Living without a partner meant plenty of time for streaming movies.

"Am I not providing you with enough entertainment?" Blair took a spot on the couch next to her.

"Oh, no. You've been pretty spectacular in that department." Rachel chuckled as she kissed her lightly.

She let the tingle pulse through her, still amazed at the effect Rachel had on her. "Good morning."

"You have good taste in movies." Rachel scrolled through the multiple action-adventure movies. "Most of these are on my favorites list too."

"So, our compatibility reaches beyond sex and food?" They'd completely agreed on what to order for dinner last night.

"Seems that way."

"Do you want to watch something?"

Rachel shook her head and clicked off the TV, then dropped the remote onto the side table. "Just passing the time until you opened your beautiful eyes."

"You should've woken me."

"I tried. You sleep like the dead."

She laughed. "I've had a lot of activity to induce that response lately. You're kinda insatiable."

"Right back atcha." Rachel moved in for a steaming kiss.

Now that was a proper good morning. "What's on your agenda for today?"

"I need to go back to the hotel."

"Oh. Right. You probably need to attend some of the conference sessions."

"No." Rachel shook her head. "That's not it." She blew out a breath. "I never intended to go to the conference after I presented, but I didn't expect to end up here either." She smiled. "I need to shower and change into some fresh clothes."

"No need for that." She peeked inside her robe. "You look fabulous without any clothes."

"You're really good for my ego. You know that?"

"I'm here to please. I'll throw something into the slow cooker for dinner."

"Am I coming back here later?"

"If you want." She was suddenly nervous. What if Rachel was done with her? "I mean, I'd like it if you would." It was a bad idea, but she wanted to spend more time with Rachel. Even if it was only for one more day. She really enjoyed Rachel's company, and the sex was off the charts. If she couldn't get her to sleep at her place, she wasn't above asking Rachel if she could stay with her at the hotel tonight.

"I don't know. I don't want to put you out. I have an early flight."

"It's no trouble. I promise not to keep you up all night and to have you to the airport on time."

"Are you sure you can keep that promise?"

"No." She shook her head. "But I'll do my best."

Rachel kissed her. "I can sleep on the plane."

CHAPTER TEN

R achel loaded her carry-on into the trunk of Blair's car before she slid into the passenger seat. She took her phone from her bag and discovered the battery was dead. "Do you have a charger I can use?" She held her cell phone up for Blair to see.

Blair opened her console and pointed to the wire plugged into the USB port inside.

"Thanks." As the phone came to life, it immediately pinged several times. She had a couple of texts from Shay and a missed call from her mom. She cleared the notifications from the screen, and the phone rang in her hand. Her mother again. "It's my mom. Do you mind?"

"No. Absolutely answer it."

"Hi, Mom."

"Are you okay? I haven't heard from you all weekend."

"I'm fine. My battery died."

"Are you still out of town?"

"Heading to the airport now."

"How was the conference?"

"Great." She smiled at Blair. "Exhilarating, in fact."

"Good. Come here when you get in. I'm making your favorite dinner."

"You didn't have to do that. I can grab something on the way home." Rachel had planned to do nothing but sleep.

"My food is better for you. Call me when you're on your way."

"Okay."

"I love you." Her mom's voice lilted up.

"I love you too." She hit the end button on her phone. "Sorry about that."

"Your mom's fixing you dinner?"

"Yeah. Feeding her children when they get home from trips is kind of a ritual of hers." And was usually greatly appreciated. Whatever sleep she got on the plane would have to do.

"That's one of the sweetest things I've ever heard." Blair grinned. "Mine hates to cook."

"Is that why you like to?"

Blair nodded. "Self-taught from my grandmother's cookbooks and a few newer ones."

"You're exceptionally good at it, among other things." She reached over and held Blair's hand.

"Well, thank you." She watched a blush overtake Blair's face.

Suddenly they were pulling up to the departure area at the airport. The ride was shorter than she'd expected. "Thank you for bringing me here." She squeezed Blair's hand and released it.

"Thank you for an unexpectedly wonderful weekend." Blair stared at her—seemed to be waiting for more.

She fumbled with the door handle as she got out of the car. Blair had already popped the trunk so she could retrieve her bag. Blair launched out of the car and beat her to the back to drag it out. She closed the trunk and stood staring, her long auburn hair blowing in the wind. Again, she seemed to be waiting for something more. Such a striking woman. Her dark green eyes burned into her, but all Rachel could focus on were her lush, full lips. She had no words for this last good-bye. "I should go. Security will probably be busy." She turned and headed to the sliding doors.

"Wait." She heard the word from behind and spun around to see Blair heading her way with intent. "I really had a great time with you this weekend." Blair took her into her arms and kissed her one last time.

All the bells and whistles went off all the way to her toes. Rachel was fully aware of her attraction to Blair sexually, but that one simple act affected her in an indescribable way. She hadn't expected a spectacular weekend affair when she'd been thinking this might be her lucky weekend, but this kiss certainly had made that possibility a reality.

"How's your neck?" She swept her fingers across it and let them land on Blair's shoulder.

"It's wonderful. No kinks at all. That tool you have is magical."

She'd bought a new massage gun from one of the vendors at the conference and planned to use it to replace the dying one in her office. But she'd left it for Blair to find when she got home. It had come in handy last night when Blair twisted the wrong way and her neck let her know it. She'd been sweet—hadn't said a word about it until she'd finished pushing Rachel over the edge for the umpteenth time. The woman was a treasure in bed, and her company was pretty good too.

"You remember the exercises I showed you, right?"

"I do." Blair mimicked the motions. "I'm sad that my personal massage therapist is leaving, though." She smiled lightly.

She rifled through her bag, wrote her cell number on the only piece of paper she could find, and handed it to Blair before she gave her one final kiss. "It was a wonderful weekend." She turned and headed through the sliding doors into the airport without looking back. Why had she given Blair her number? This could be only a weekend of her life—one that would never happen again.

Slot-machine bells rang as Rachel zoomed through the airport to security. She had TSA-Pre, so all she had to do was drop her bag onto the rollers and push it through the X-ray scanner. Nothing beeped as she walked through the metal-detector cage, so she was good to go. Only she wasn't really.

Her feelings confused her. She needed to leave this affair in Las Vegas, but the urge to give Blair her number had been too strong. She wanted to see her again—come back soon to continue what they'd started.

❖

Blair's stomach knotted as she watched Rachel walk into the airport before she got into her car. She'd tried to stay cool, but she hadn't been able to stop herself from kissing Rachel one last time.

She'd gone all in this weekend, even skipping a day of work, which she didn't do often. She'd never be able to meet her financial goal if she did. The knot in her stomach tightened. Even though it had been a spectacular weekend, she had no future with someone who wouldn't provide any geographical information about herself. She'd given Rachel several chances, but she deflected each time. Blair fired the engine and put the car into gear. This was the closest to love she'd felt in a long time, but now she had to let the feeling go.

CHAPTER ELEVEN

Rachel arrived safely back in Florida, sped through the airport, and took the shuttle to the long-term parking lot. She'd slept through most of the flight, but now she just wanted to go home and crawl into bed. The weekend had been wonderful—so much more than she'd expected—but also exhausting. She drove on autopilot to her parents' house.

She'd felt sad as she sat in the airport waiting for her flight. Even with hundreds of people surrounding her, she'd never felt so lonely. She'd never expected to meet anyone on this last-minute trip, and she certainly hadn't expected to connect with anyone the way she had with Blair. The only other person she'd ever felt that with was Shay, and realistically nothing would ever happen between them—unless Shay screwed up again. And if that happened, would she really want to be with a woman who couldn't remain faithful?

After she pulled up to her parents' home, she flipped the visor mirror open and fixed her makeup, adding some coverup to the circles under her eyes before she went inside. If she didn't, her mom would notice, and she wasn't up for a discussion tonight on taking better care of herself.

She let herself in as usual. Her parents maintained a welcoming household. Many friends of hers and her siblings had crossed this threshold in the past. Her family had taken in some friends who'd been raised under horrible circumstances and embraced them as their own. She doubted that would ever change.

Her mom stood in the kitchen taking baked chicken and rice from the oven—one of her childhood favorites. Even though she'd tried to make the dish on her own, no one could make it quite like her mother.

"This is wonderful. Thank you, Mom." This morning when she was trying to talk her mother out of this meal, she hadn't realized how much she needed this welcome home. "Where's Dad?"

"He had a dinner meeting with a client." Her dad was a corporate attorney and worked late most days. "How was your trip?"

"It was okay." A shiver shot through her as she remembered the night before. What was she thinking? She wasn't the wild-girl type. She didn't have torrid affairs with women she barely knew, yet she'd embroiled herself in one with Blair over the weekend and had reveled in it.

"Your presentation went well?"

"Yes." She had to get Blair out of her head. "Absolutely. Lots of people said they enjoyed it."

"How is your friend?"

"My friend?" She hadn't mentioned Blair, had she?

"The one from work who got sick."

"Oh. Amy. I haven't heard. I need to check on her." She took out her phone and typed in a quick text.

How are you feeling?

A response from Amy came back quickly. *Better. I can eat now.*

That's good to hear. We don't want you getting any thinner than you already are.

Bubbles appeared on the screen, and a laugh emoji appeared.

"She's better." She swallowed, her throat dry, hopefully due only to the flight.

"I'll pack her some chicken and rice, and you can drop it off on your way home."

"Sure." She would take it tomorrow instead. No use arguing about it.

She finished the last bit of rice on her plate and began clearing the table. "That was so good."

Her mom beamed. "Still your favorite?"

"Still my favorite." She kissed her cheek.

As she was loading the dishwasher, her phone chimed. Probably Amy again, or Shay checking to see if she'd gotten home safely. She'd been bad about replying to Shay this weekend. She picked up her phone to check, but the text was from Blair.

When are you coming back? Blair had added a sad face, a broken heart, and a surprise-face emoji at the end.

She laughed at the emojis, but they hit home—she was feeling the same way. She'd spent only a weekend with Blair, but it felt like a lifetime. She hesitated to text back. Nothing could really come of whatever had happened between them except their weekend rendezvous in Vegas—could it?

Another message came through. *We didn't even get a chance to go dancing.* Several dancing emojis followed before a disco gif appeared.

She typed in a message. *I want more pancakes.* She found the pancake emoji and added it. They had hardly slept their last night together and had been up early making breakfast together.

She waited for the next message—watched the text bubbles. A string of food emojis appeared. *We have so much more to do in the kitchen…and the living room…and the bedroom.*

The improbability of that happening made her a little sad. Two thousand miles was a lot for a long-distance relationship.

YOU are a genius in all those areas. The sex had been phenomenal.

She immediately received a blush-face emoji.

"Who are you texting so furiously?" Her mother looked over at the screen.

"It's just work." She typed in one last text.

I have to go. At my mom's for dinner.

Oh, yeah. I forgot. Can we talk later?

She didn't answer, unsure where she should go with this and what it actually was. She probably shouldn't have given Blair her number. She needed to leave this one in Vegas. She just didn't know how to let Blair go—wasn't sure she was ready to.

❖

Once Rachel got home, she went into her bedroom and tossed her suitcase onto the bed to unpack. When she unzipped her bag, she immediately focused on Blair's robe, which was folded neatly and placed on top of her clothing just under the suitcase straps. When had Blair slipped that in? She picked it up and held it to her nose, and a note fell from it to the floor.

You looked so good in this, I thought you should have it.
It will help you remember me until next time...
Thank you for a wonderful weekend.

Every bit of that was true, except the first line, but she didn't need help remembering Blair. Their time together would be forever burned into her memory. It might have been easier if everything hadn't been so perfect—if they hadn't been so in sync. Even though they seemed to gel in every way, it was unrealistic to feel like she'd found her perfect match in one weekend.

She stripped her clothes off and tossed them into the hamper before she slipped on the robe and got into bed. She clicked on the TV, found the show they'd been watching together, and started the next episode.

Her phone chimed, and when she picked it up and saw the text was from Shay, she was weirdly disappointed it wasn't from Blair, even though she hadn't planned to respond to her.

You make it home okay?

Home and in bed.

How was your trip? The conference? I didn't hear from you much.

Busy. Lots of great activities.

That wasn't a lie. She'd been very busy with Blair, but she would keep that do herself for now. She wasn't sure if embarrassment was holding her back or the fact that she was still hung up on Shay and didn't want her to know. It wasn't like Blair lived here in Tampa. How would she even tell Shay? Guilt began to set in, and she shrugged it off. *I'm entitled to a life, aren't I?*

She tugged the collar of the robe Blair had given her to her nose and breathed in her sweet scent, remembered how special she'd made her feel. She would ride out this comfort for a few more days before she buried the loss of it in her closet.

CHAPTER TWELVE

B lair was in her bedroom getting ready for her shift at the casino bar when her phone rang. She took it from the dresser, saw that it was Tess, her closest friend and confidant, and immediately answered and put the call on speaker.

"Hey there. I wasn't expecting to hear from you today."

"Why not?" Tess's voice lilted up.

"I don't know. I thought you'd be busy with work. Taking clients to dinner, schmoozing into the wee hours of the night."

"Nope. That gets old real fast. Tonight, Sophie and I are eating in and watching a movie."

"Good luck with that. She'll be asleep before you get halfway through it."

Tess laughed her sweet, innocent laugh. "Spot-on."

At first, Blair had been bitter about being used as a jealousy factor between them, but in the end, when it all shook out, she realized it hadn't been intentional. She really couldn't hold the whole falling-in-love-with-Sophie thing against Tess. They were a perfect match. Although Blair had tried to avoid her, Tess had persisted in her quest for friendship, and now she didn't know how she'd ever have done without her positive attitude.

"So how many weeks until you're back home?"

"Not long. Ten days. I'm counting them down." She glanced around the room looking for her black, rubber-soled loafers and spotted one of them next to the bed. "I can't wait to get out of here and back into my own place." She knelt, reached under the bed, and located the other shoe, then slipped both on.

"I thought you liked the house you rented from your aunt."

"I do, but it's just not home. I can't put a nail in the wall without asking her," she shouted as she went into the closet and changed into her black, button-down shirt. "Well, I can, but I don't feel comfortable making any changes without telling her."

"I get that."

Rachel popped into her head. She sank onto the bed, ran her hand across the pillowcase. Should she spill to Tess about her amazing weekend with someone she'd probably never see again? "I met a woman last week." The words were out of her mouth before she could stop them.

"Oh? That's great. Does she live in Vegas?"

"No. She was a guest at the hotel." The vision of her walking out of registration into the bar flashed through her mind. She'd seemed so unattainable then.

"And?"

"And we spent the most fabulous weekend together."

"That's wonderful, right?"

"It was pretty awesome." She warmed as the memory of Rachel's smile filled her thoughts. "She's gone home now, and I have no idea where that is."

"She didn't tell you?"

"No. She avoided the subject whenever I brought it up." She hadn't outright asked her, though.

"Can you find out from the registration desk?"

"No. They won't give out that kind of information. It's cause for termination."

"Well, shit."

"Right? I finally find someone I really click with and have no idea where to find her." She had Rachel's number, but since her last text had gone unanswered, she didn't plan to send more. Her ego was fragile enough already.

"I didn't realize people took those rules about Vegas seriously."

"Yeah. Things can get pretty wild here. Enough about me. How are things going there?"

"Actually. I just contracted to display a few of my photographs in a gallery."

"That's great. Where is it?"

"It's actually in Tampa. The owner was looking for help with her advertising and found us online."

"Cool. So, it's a mutual thing?"

"Not at first, but when she found out I was into photography, she asked to see it, and now I'm going to show in *her* gallery."

"You can't ask for more than that."

"Well, I can, but it's a little soon to ask for great sales and fame." Tess laughed.

"Like you would ever want to be famous. Your face turns red when anyone praises you."

"Right? Can I just show it and not have to talk to anyone?"

"That's not the way it works. Besides, you talk to people all the time." Tess was a great conversationalist. Otherwise, she would never have convinced Blair to remain friends with her.

"I know, but this is personal. I don't know if I'll be able to stand the reviews."

"Then don't read them."

"It's tough not to."

"Okay. I'll read them first and then deliver them to you. I'm up for hearing about your greatness." She would also give shitty reviewers a piece of her mind. Some people were just full of meanness. She'd learned that from some of the comments left in response to her poetry in the bill books at The Speak Easy.

"Deal."

She glanced at her watch. "Hey, can I call you back later or tomorrow? I have to get moving, or I'll be late for work."

"You bet. Talk to you soon. I can't wait until you're back home again."

"Me either. Bye." She hit the end button and slid her phone into her back pocket. After rushing into the kitchen, she tossed a couple packages of peanut-butter crackers into her bag and hurried out the door.

Blair stood behind the horseshoe bar and watched as people came out of the registration area. She was mixing drinks on autopilot tonight. Just a week ago she'd met Rachel, the woman who'd totally turned her life upside down—at least for a weekend. She should've asked more questions, found out where she lived, tried to see if they could make a long-distance thing work.

"Hey. Where's your mind at tonight?" Morgan set a martini in front of her. "This should be a Gibson." She plucked the toothpick of olives out of the drink and replaced it with one of pearl onions.

She scrunched her eyebrows together. "Sorry. I must've misunderstood." This wasn't good. She was becoming obsessed.

While Morgan took the drink to the customer at the other end of the bar, she slid her phone from her back pocket and scrolled through her text messages. She pulled up the string with Rachel, and her stomach knotted. Her last message was still unanswered—radio silence from Rachel. She tucked her phone back into her pocket. Clearly, she was making more of their time together than it was. It was a weekend in Vegas, that was all. A really great weekend in a town where people want to remain anonymous. *What happens in Vegas...stays in Vegas.* She needed to remember that saying.

"Can a lady get a drink around here?" The familiar voice pulled her from her thoughts, and she knew immediately who it was. She'd been avoiding the woman for months. No sense trying any longer. She glanced over her shoulder and smiled. That had been the first mistake she'd made when she got to Vegas, the reason she was so careful about who she socialized with now.

"Hey, there." She reached for the vodka. "The usual?"

The woman nodded as she watched her rim the glass with sugar.

She poured vodka, Cointreau, lemon juice, and simple syrup into the shaker and gave it a healthy shake to mix before she strained it into the martini glass. She hung a lemon twist on the side and slid the drink in front of her.

"I came by to see you Saturday night."

"I was home. I've been sick." A half-truth.

"If I'd known, I would've brought you some soup." The woman stared as she touched her drink to her lips.

"I appreciate that. Just needed some rest." One night of horrible sex had led to multiple phone calls and texts. When she'd blocked the woman on her phone, she'd started showing up unannounced at the bar. She had her well-meaning aunt to thank for that. She was a friend of a friend's daughter who, according to her aunt, was the sweetest lesbian she'd ever met. Her aunt couldn't understand why she didn't have a girlfriend. Blair had become intimately acquainted with those reasons and had immediately tried to distance herself. Thankfully, they'd spent only a limited amount of time together, and it had been all at Laura's place. Was that her name, or was it Lauren? That was still a mystery to her. Perhaps she was trying to blank out the whole incident. Not telling Laura/Lauren where she lived or that she rented from her aunt was the best move she'd unintentionally made. She'd given her aunt only a few of the details and sworn her to secrecy, and she'd promised to never give out her address.

Blair had pretty much sworn off women until Rachel walked into her life. But that hadn't turned out so well either.

She squatted to get a new bottle of vodka from the cabinet behind her.

Morgan appeared beside her as she shifted the bottles. "Got any gin in there?"

She handed her a bottle. "Want to make a wager on Laurie?" She was joking about the wager, but she would love for Morgan to take her off her hands.

"You mean Lana?" Wow, she was way off on that one. "Uh-uh. That problem's all yours." Morgan grinned. "She was here looking for you last weekend."

"What'd you tell her?"

"That you were sick. You were, weren't you?" Morgan raised her eyebrows.

"Yes. I'm still a bit raspy." She coughed into her hand. "Can't you tell?" She *had* been sick, but her sore throat hadn't turned up until Tuesday morning, and she'd been off work all week. She'd caught strep throat, probably from Rachel, which had set her back some financially, but, just the same, she was determined to stick with her plan to move in a couple of weeks. She'd thought a lot about it while she was in bed sick, and alone. She wanted to go home.

Her phone buzzed in her pocket. She took it out and looked at the screen. A FaceTime call from Tess. "I need to take this. Can you handle things for a few minutes?"

Morgan nodded. "Sure."

She moved through the bar flipper, walked into the small seating area next to the bar, and sat in one of the velvet club chairs. "Hey, there. Do you know your timing is impeccable?"

"Oh yeah? What's going on?"

"Just avoiding the usual unwanted guest at the bar."

"Is she still coming around?" Tess's voice rose.

"Yep. Front and center." She glanced at the bar. "Watching me right now. Who knew I would have my very own stalker?"

"That's creepy. You should notify security."

"She's harmless—obsessed, but harmless. Besides, she'll be a non-issue once I move back to Florida." She shifted to face the other way. "Anyway. How's the opening going?"

"It's been so busy." Tess flipped the camera to scan her photography displayed on the wall. "I've already sold a few."

"Wow. You have a whole wall to yourself?"

"I do. Isn't it awesome?"

"That's fantastic." She was happy for Tess. She was such a good person and deserved to be happy—rewarded in all she did. When she'd told Tess about her dream of owning her own mobile bar, she'd helped her write a business plan and encouraged her to make it happen. Blair was fairly certain she'd still be tending bar and trying to figure out her life without Tess's support.

The picture flipped back to Tess. "Gotta go. Sophie is waving me down."

"Enjoy your night."

Tess smiled widely. "I will. Call you tomorrow." The screen went black.

She headed back to the bar and was immediately met with a wide smile from her uninvited guest. She went straight to Morgan. "Come on. Do a girl a solid and switch sides with me?" They did this when one of them was uncomfortable with a guest.

"Okay, but don't blame me when she slides around to the other side."

They were going to get pretty dizzy tonight.

CHAPTER THIRTEEN

Rachel was staring into her computer monitor trying to catch up on her charting when a knock on the door made her pulse jump. "Come in." She glanced up from the screen. "Hi." She was surprised to see Chloe come through the door.

"Hi. Sorry to drop in on you like this." Chloe stopped. "You cut your hair."

"Yeah." She threaded her fingers through it. "I needed a change." She needed to get herself out of this funk she was in since she'd returned home from Las Vegas. The haircut hadn't helped.

"Do you have a couple of minutes to chat?"

"Sure. Want to go to the cafeteria and get some coffee?"

"No. I'm good. Unless you want to."

She shook her head. "There's water in the mini-fridge over there." She pointed to the corner where it stood.

Chloe went to the refrigerator and took out a bottle before she sat down in the chair beside the desk. "Listen. Shay's behavior Friday night surprised me. I know you two are friends, but it seems like she's becoming more attached to you." Chloe sucked in a deep breath. "Is anything going on between you two?"

"Absolutely not." She definitely had feelings for Shay, but she'd done her best to keep them in check. Everything between them was totally platonic. "She's made it perfectly clear that she's in love with you." She couldn't compete with the love of Shay's life.

"It's none of my business, but when is the last time you dated?"

Thoughts of Blair filled her head. "You're right. It's none of your business."

"Understood." Chloe tightened her lips and stood.

"I'm sorry. Please sit back down. I met someone in Las Vegas and had..." She shook her head. "I'm not sure exactly what it was, but it was the most fun I've had with another woman in a long time."

"You met someone?" Chloe grinned like she'd just sold her most expensive piece of art. "Are you going to see her again?"

"I don't know." She really didn't. "We didn't talk about it, and she lives in Las Vegas. Long distance isn't the best scenario for something new."

"Vegas flights are cheap, though."

"Yeah, but I'm not really keen on the four-hour flight time."

"You can always meet in the middle somewhere, and there's always FaceTime."

"Traveling can get expensive." She wasn't counting on anything more from her weekend affair, even though she and Blair seemed to get along perfectly, and the sex was ridiculously hot.

"So, tell me about her."

"She's sweet and funny."

"How did you meet her? Was she attending the conference?"

"No." She shook her head. "She's a bartender at the hotel."

"You just randomly hooked up with a bartender? That doesn't sound like something you'd do."

"No." Since when did Chloe have any idea what she'd do? "We chatted for a bit at the bar the night I got in, and she was working there again the next night." *Then we randomly hooked up.* Heat filled her. *Did we ever.*

"And?"

"And the next day I went on a winery excursion and ran into her again." She wasn't sure why she was telling Chloe all this.

Chloe pulled her eyebrows together. "She followed you? That's kind of creepy."

"No. She works there too." She hadn't planned to see her again at all. "It was kind of awkward seeing her there."

"Wow. That seems a little serendipitous—that she was everywhere you were."

"Seemed like it." She sighed. "She gave me a personal tour of the winery before she found someone to cover her shift, and then we went on a day-long adventure to the vineyard and then sightseeing." *Bought me dinner and did so much more.* "We had a great weekend. Just fun and easy, enjoying each other's company."

"I'm glad to hear that. It's too bad she doesn't live here."

"Yeah." Rachel pulled her eyebrows together. "Can I ask you something?"

Chloe laughed. "Well, how can I refuse after I just grilled you about your weekend?"

"Why do you let me come around if you know I have feelings for Shay?"

"To be honest, I don't relish seeing you all doe-eyed around her, but you're her friend, and she's partial to your company. I won't take that away from her. Not after all we've been through."

"Sorry. I didn't realize I'm that transparent. You're awfully understanding."

"I'm not gonna lie." Chloe shook her head. "I worry about it, but Shay has a mind of her own, and it's not like I can stop her from being your friend. After all, you did help bring her back to me."

She'd helped Shay recover her strength through many hours of physical therapy, only to have her regain her memory of the breaking point—where her relationship with Chloe had been at the time of the accident. When she'd seen how devastated Shay was about losing her marriage, Rachel knew there was no chance for her. Shay had been deeply in love with Chloe—still was.

Chloe touched her hand. "I'm glad to hear you connected with someone, even if it was random and you might never see her again. But if you really want to be happy and not just someone's backup, you have to close that door in your heart if you want a new one to open."

Everything Chloe said was spot-on, but letting go was difficult. She'd had a great weekend in Las Vegas, hadn't really thought about Shay at all, but now she was back to reality, and her love life in Florida was nonexistent.

CHAPTER FOURTEEN

B lair felt giddy as the delivery men brought her new bar equipment into the house and began removing the protective wrap. It had taken her a while, but she'd worked a massive amount of long, hard hours in Las Vegas to save enough money to get back home to Florida and start her bartending business. The equipment wasn't cheap, but after lots of research and much contemplation, she'd decided on a sixty-inch-wide, thirty-five-inch deep, zero-step cockpit design. It was designed to speed up the number of drinks a bartender poured by keeping everything within reach. If she was working alone, moving back and forth too much could be hell on her feet. The bar was made of molded polyethylene and aluminum composite material, both highly resistant to corrosion for working outdoors near the water and practically impervious to dings and dents. It wasn't cheap, and she'd had to factor the price of a used full-size van to transport it into her budget as well. She'd miss her Mustang, but it was well worth the trade.

"How did you afford to buy all this equipment?" Morgan asked.

"I worked my ass off and haven't gone out at all the past year." She ran her hand across the inlaid perforated workboard on the bar top. "I also took out a small-business loan to cover some of the more expensive items." She'd already purchased a Boston shaker and Hawthorne strainer, as well as a jigger, cutting board, paring knife, and multiple other necessary accessories. The cost seemed to add up quickly. Next up would be stocking it with alcohol—a hefty price tag in itself. She'd need that only for small private parties or if she branched out and bought a mobile trailer. Most events supplied their own liquor. She pulled off the remaining protective wrap and squatted before she stared at the logo imprinted on the front. *Blissful Bubbles.* The giddy feeling hit her again, and she couldn't believe it was all hers.

"I guess I should look into doing that myself."

"What happened to your idea of finding your sugar mama to support you?"

"I've been reconsidering that possibility. I want to be in control of my own destiny, and that situation gives someone else too much power over me." Morgan slid her hand over the bar. "I'm available if you need an extra hand."

"Your day job not keeping you busy enough?" Morgan had taken a job interning at SoTess Marketing, Tess and Sophie's new advertising company that they'd formed after the whole awkward weekend at the Palm Beach Club Resort when they'd all met face to face. Blair was so grateful to her close friend, Tess, for helping her with so many things to make this dream of hers happen.

"It's busy, but I'm still an intern, so the pay isn't all that great." Morgan frowned.

"Thanks. I can't pay you much either."

"No one ever does. I survive on tips." This situation was common in the service industry.

"I have an extra room for rent if you need it." Blair raised her eyebrows. She could use the extra money as well.

Morgan shook her head. "No. I'm good. Since Sophie moved in with Tess, she's letting me live at her place while I intern for them." The mention of that arrangement didn't make Blair's stomach clench anymore. Even though she'd ended up being a pawn between Tess and Sophie, she was actually happy they were together now and couldn't see either of them with herself or anyone else.

"Okay. Then you can be my second in command. First event is in the arts district." It was just over thirty minutes' travel time. Although she'd lived in Orlando previously, she'd chosen to live on the outskirts of Lakeland, closer to the interstate, so she could take advantage of both the Tampa and Orlando markets.

"You got that one?"

"Yep. Thanks to recommendations from you and Tess." It didn't hurt that the gallery had been struggling to find a reliable portable bar service.

"I don't know Chloe all that well, but Tess says she's really nice and easy to get along with. She handles the events but lets someone else manage the day-to-day activities at the gallery."

"I can imagine handling multiple artists would be stressful." At least as stressful as running a bar business.

"Have you seen Tess's photography yet?"

"She FaceTimed me during her first event. The place was packed." She smiled as she remembered Tess's excitement. "She could hardly contain herself."

"She promised to help me with my design photos." Morgan pinched her lips together. "If I ever get back to school." Morgan had planned to go to clothing-design school in Georgia.

"What's that about? I mean, why did you decide not to go back right now?"

"School is harder than I expected. I just need to take some time and regroup—decide what I really want to do for the rest of my life."

"Well, it looks like Tess and Sophie like having you around."

"I *do* like working there. They listen to my input too, which is refreshing."

"So why don't you go into advertising with them? I'm sure they can use your sense of style and design."

"I've thought about it, but I want to make sure. Don't want to change my mind after I've committed. That wouldn't be good for any of us."

"True. That's probably a smart plan."

"What about you? Are you going to do this for the rest of your life?" Morgan motioned to the bar equipment.

"I hope to expand—hire other people and eventually run the business rather than the bar." She continued checking her inventory. "If that doesn't happen in the next five years, I'll have to reconsider." She really hoped she could succeed. Otherwise, she'd end up working for someone else again.

❖

Rachel glanced at the clock when Amy, her counterpart in the PT department and second in command, rushed in just before noon, as usual. The physical-therapy department was open until eight o'clock during the week to accommodate patients who worked nine-to-five jobs, and she worked the later shift. "I brought doughnuts."

"How about sandwiches? It's lunchtime."

"Not for me." Amy grinned and dropped the box on the table just outside the office door. "Is there fresh coffee?" She plucked a glazed doughnut out, bit into it, then closed her eyes and indulged in the treat.

"Yep." Rachel had stopped drinking an hour ago, but she'd just made a fresh pot because Amy always needed coffee when she arrived. She stood and poured Amy a cup from the pot set up on top of the mini refrigerator in the corner of the office.

"You should really have one of these. They're still hot." She talked as she chewed. "I bought them from the twenty-four-hour shop." Amy opened the box and turned it her way. "I got your favorite."

She went to the table and stared at the maple Long John. "That's really not fair, you know." She picked it up and took a bite. "You're going to ruin my lunch."

"My goal for the day." Amy closed the box and glanced around the room as she sipped her coffee. "Anything out of the ordinary schedule I need to know about?"

"New patient coming in at twelve thirty." She poured herself a cup of coffee. "Teenager with a shattered ankle from a car accident. Should be just about done getting the cast off now."

"Oh, good. Teenagers are fun." They weren't always, but Amy had a way of making them see the brighter side of therapy. She had a way of doing that for most people, even with all the stooping, bending, and other physical work she performed on the daily.

Physical therapy was difficult for both the therapist and the patient—hours filled with plenty of activity and hard work—but the rewards were great. Seeing someone recover from life-changing injuries provided the best feeling. Being able to help people improve their lives and physical health on a daily basis was a true gift.

Her phone rang, and she glanced at the screen. "I need to get this." She picked up the phone as she rounded the desk. "Hey there."

"Hey. How's your day going?" Shay's voice was as soft and sweet as always.

"Good, so far. Although I'm about to go into a sugar high."

"What?"

"Amy brought doughnuts." She glanced up and smiled at her.

"Now I wish I'd come by instead of calling."

"We still have some left, and they're *really* good."

"I can't get away. My brother's on vacation, and I've been skipping lunch to keep up so I can get out of here early Friday. Will you be available to escort me to the gallery?" Shay was still chief actuary at an insurance company and worked long hours, on occasion, even though she'd promoted her brother and her assistant, and shifted some of the workload to them.

"Of course. As always."

"Great." The phone call became muffled. "I'm sorry. I have to go, but I'll call you later."

The call ended before she could respond. She was usually delighted to hear from Shay at any time, but being cut off so quickly irritated her. Were Shay's calls with Chloe that clipped? She dropped her phone to the desk.

"Was that Shay?"

"How could you tell?"

"You went from happy to sad, as you always do when she calls." Amy stood across the desk from her. "Why do you still want her?"

She shrugged. "It's not a matter of want. I don't know how to get her out of my head."

"Date someone else." Amy enunciated the words pointedly.

She'd done that, sorta, in Las Vegas. "It's not that easy finding someone."

"Sure, it is. There are tons of dating platforms out there now. Tinder, Match, Zoosk, and Elite, just to name a few."

"I don't want to do that. It's too much work, and it's awkward meeting new people." Yet she hadn't felt awkward at all with Blair.

"What about Be Naughty? You can just have fun without commitment."

"No. Absolutely not. A lot of weirdos out there just want to have fun." Maybe she was the weirdo.

"Okay then. I'll find you someone."

"I don't want that either. I just want to meet someone naturally."

"Too late. I'm going to start working on it now." Amy picked up her phone and started scrolling through her social media.

An attendant came through the door, pushing the new patient in a wheelchair. "This is the physical-therapy department, where you get your ankle back into working order."

Amy slipped her phone into her back pocket. "We'll continue this later."

"Not if I can help it." She'd had a lot of fun with Blair in Las Vegas, but the thought of putting herself back into the dating pool scared her.

CHAPTER FIFTEEN

At the gallery First Friday event, Blair was thankful for Morgan's help. Getting the bar out of the van was easy, but carrying it up the steps and into the gallery required muscle, and Morgan had plenty of that. The line for drinks was getting thick, and more people were entering the gallery by the minute. The two of them were handling the thirsty crowd well. They were there to keep people happy because happy people spent more money on art.

"What a great night, huh?" Morgan was just as excited as Blair was about their success.

Blair took a breath during the momentary lull. Many more people were there than she'd estimated. "I need to go out to the van. We're running low on vodka." They hadn't started with a full bottle, and she'd forgotten to bring in the spare. The owner of the gallery had chosen not to supply her own alcohol for this event.

"I'll get it." Morgan held her hand out, waiting for the keys.

Blair checked her black V-neck blouse and then glanced around the gallery. She didn't see a familiar face in the room besides Tess, Sophie, and Chloe, the owner. They were all camped out in front of a wall covered with Tess's photography, talking to two other women with short, dark hair. One was a little taller than the other, dressed in similar blue slacks and collared shirts—one blue, the other red—and both looked a bit butch from behind. Maybe tonight would be her lucky night in more ways than one.

The group of women turned and headed her way. She began preparing the usual drinks for Tess, Sophie, and Chloe, the three she knew from earlier. When she looked up to set them on the bar, she was stunned, and Rachel seemed to be as well. She'd cut her hair, but Blair could never forget that beautiful face. A thrill shot through her.

Chloe's voice broke the connection. "I don't believe you've met my wife, Shay." Chloe rubbed Shay's shoulder. "And this is her friend Rachel."

"Nice to meet you." Rachel smiled and held out her hand.

She shook it—held it tightly. "Have we met before?"

"No. I don't think so."

Blair's heart sank. She felt like she'd just been gut-punched. How could Rachel not even acknowledge her—not give her the slightest bit of recognition after the spectacular weekend they'd spent together? Obviously, it hadn't had the same impact on Rachel as it had on her.

Shay reached out next. "Chloe says you're a fantastic mixologist."

"I do my best." She put the three drinks she'd already mixed on the bar. "What can I make for you?"

"A glass of white wine for me." Shay smiled at Rachel. "I'm a lightweight."

She filled the plastic glass with wine and pushed it across the bar to Shay before she popped open a beer and set it on the counter in front of Rachel. "You look like a beer drinker."

"She sure pegged you." Shay grinned and clinked her glass against Rachel's beer bottle.

"Looks like it." Rachel avoided eye contact.

Morgan came back behind the bar, and Blair hooked her arm around her. "This is Morgan, my partner." She didn't know why she'd said it—only that she was confused, hurt, and angry, and she needed to make Rachel aware of her feelings.

Rachel snapped her gaze to hers and flitted her eyelids. It seemed she did have some feelings after all. It was disappointing that she couldn't be transparent about them.

Morgan pulled her closer, taking advantage of the situation since she seemed to sense what was happening. Their *partnership* was nothing more than professional.

She observed the close proximity Rachel kept to Shay and realized that she might be the woman Rachel was in love with. But that was an impossible situation since Shay was married to Chloe.

"You look familiar. Have we met?" Morgan asked.

"No. I don't believe so. Unless you've worked the bar here before."

"No. Can't be that." Morgan glanced at Blair. "This is our first time here." She stared at Rachel again. "Anyway. We're here if you need another beer."

They both watched as the group of women strolled to another area of the gallery.

"Hang on." Morgan gave Blair a sideways glance. "Wasn't that the woman you met a couple of weeks ago in Vegas? The one you spent the weekend with?"

She nodded. "Yeah. She cut her hair. I didn't recognize her at first." She should have, after all the time she'd spend exploring her body.

Morgan scrunched her eyebrows. "I can't believe she didn't remember you." She grabbed her arm and widened her eyes. "Wait. Did she just blow you off?"

Blair shrugged. "I guess I wasn't that memorable." Such a lie... their encounter would be burned into her memory for the rest of time, and she was certain it would be that way for Rachel as well.

"I don't believe that for a minute. Jesus, you have shitty luck with women."

"You're not wrong about that." She shook her head and chuckled as she tried to contain her pain.

Soon after that, Rachel and Shay went through the front door and sat at one of the tables in front of the gallery. She watched them intently, Rachel laughing and smiling as she interacted with Shay. She didn't look through the window—hadn't even glanced back as she'd left the bar. Shay was definitely the woman she couldn't let go—a married woman.

Rachel hadn't planned to return to the gallery tonight, but she'd acted so badly earlier and felt Blair deserved an explanation—at least an apology. She'd felt Blair's stare burning into her back as she quickly made her way across the gallery with Shay, then outside to one of the small tables. When she'd peeped through the glass, she'd found that the bar was busy again, and Blair was all business, making drinks. Surprised and embarrassed, she didn't know what had come over her or why she'd acted like they were strangers. She didn't usually jump right into bed with women—and never did one-night stands—or weekend stands in this case. Although Rachel hadn't told Shay directly, she suspected Chloe had already mentioned the woman she'd met in Las Vegas. That tidbit of news had made Chloe extremely happy. She wasn't sure she wanted to divulge all the details of what had happened with Blair, and Shay apparently didn't want to hear them, or she would've already said something.

She could see the excitement in Blair's eyes when they'd connected with hers and then watched it dim when she pretended not to know her. How could she have done that after the spectacular weekend they'd shared? During the whole flight home, she'd wished Blair lived closer, and now here she was, and she'd fucked the whole thing up.

The front gallery door was locked, with no movement inside. She walked around the building and found Blair alone behind the gallery, loading the last of her equipment. "Where's your partner?"

"She took off already." Blair didn't look at her. "She's not really my partner."

"Then why did you say she was?" She vaguely remembered her from the bar in Las Vegas.

Blair swung around and put her hand on her hip. "Why did you act like you'd never seen me before?"

"I was surprised and didn't know how to react—what to say." Blindsided was more like it.

"*It's nice to see you again* would've been a start." Blair gave her a false smile. "I guess that's not the case."

"Honestly, I never expected to see you again after we said good-bye at the airport a few weeks ago." She wasn't sure how to accept the fact that Blair was actually here in Tampa.

"That's obvious." Blair wadded up a stray bar towel and fired it into the van.

"Why didn't you tell me you were moving to Florida?"

"Didn't move. I came back. Florida is my home." Blair climbed inside the back of the van and finished tying down the portable bar.

"You didn't volunteer anything about where you live, so I didn't think you wanted to know. More important, why didn't you mention you're involved with someone else's wife?" Clearly Blair was pissed.

"I'm not." Rachel pulled her eyebrows together. Not in the way Blair was assuming.

Blair raised an eyebrow. "Don't lie to me."

She sighed. "It's complicated."

"I can see that." Blair put a box into her van and pushed it all the way forward. "Otherwise, Shay would've already known we've met before."

"I'm sorry. I was weird about it and made it awkward." She helped Blair lift another box and slide it into the back. "Let me make it up to you. Please?" She raised her eyebrows. "I owe you at least that for the spectacular time you showed me in Las Vegas."

Blair flattened her lips as she continued stowing the rest of her gear. "My reward for that weekend was a miserable case of strep throat." She tossed the last bag on top of everything else. "I lost three days of work because of it."

Rachel put her hand to her mouth. "Oh my God. I'm so sorry." She moved closer and tucked a stray strand of hair behind Blair's ear. "If it makes you feel better, I was in bed for the same when I got home. Couldn't eat *anything*." The familiar fire coursed her system as she leaned in, ready to stoke it higher with a scorching kiss.

"It doesn't." Blair stared into her eyes. "Well, maybe a little."

Blair's grin sent another jolt through her, and she moved even closer.

"Hold on." Blair bolted backward, put some distance between them. "You're not going to infect me again, are you?"

"No." She shook her head. "Clean bill of health here." Now she stared into Blair's eyes, then watched hers as they moved down, lingered on her lips before pivoting up to her eyes again.

Blair took a step forward, stroked her cheek lightly before she slid her hand slowly down to her neck and snaked it around behind it. Next came the most blistering kiss—one she'd longed for ever since she left Las Vegas. In a split second she was completely in Blair's control. She tingled as she pressed into Blair, each of her senses remembering their past experience in vivid detail. This woman did wild things to her, making her willpower puddle. Memories of Blair's screams as she launched into orgasm filled her head, and soon she had Blair pressed up against her vehicle, struggling to get her hand into her pants. She wanted her so badly—had to feel Blair's need on her fingers right now.

Blair broke the kiss and pushed her away. "That's not going to happen here." She shifted uncomfortably.

"What?" She sucked in a breath, trying to clear the fog in her brain.

"I said no." Blair's voice was low and raspy.

"Don't even try to tell me that first night in Vegas wasn't just like a dream."

"I can't do that. The whole weekend was..." Blair smiled as she shook her head slowly... "It was something I can't even begin to describe, but we're not going to do anything here...in an alley behind an art gallery." Her cheeks were red, her breathing heavy. She seemed to be affected the same way Rachel was.

"Then come home with me?" In this moment, Rachel would do anything to make that happen.

"What would people think?" Blair's voice was calm, her breathing back to normal. Clearly, she was still wounded.

"I don't care," Rachel said. But did she really not care? If Shay appeared right now, would she back off—act like a complete ass again? Possibly. She heard voices and glanced over her shoulder.

"I think you do." Blair closed the back of the van. "Why don't you think on it and call me tomorrow?" She reached into her back pocket, took out a card, and handed it to her. "In case you lost my number."

She hadn't but had forced herself not to call. She rubbed the embossed lettering between her fingers as she watched Blair get into the van and drive away. She didn't need to think. She would definitely call Blair tomorrow, but she had to figure out how to make up for her ridiculous reaction earlier.

CHAPTER SIXTEEN

It was barely seven a.m. when Blair's phone chimed. She rolled over and checked the screen. A text from Rachel. She smiled. The woman wasn't giving up, which pleased her to some extent.

Rachel: *Can we forget everything that happened and start over?*

Blair: *Not sure I can forget Vegas. Unless you have some kind of memory-wiping machine.*

Rachel: *Lol. I don't want to ever forget that.* The line was punctuated with a fire emoji.

Blair: *Yeah?* That was a relief because Blair couldn't possibly erase it from her mind.

Rachel: *Yeah. It was a pretty amazing weekend.*

Blair: *I thought so too. But last night still has me a little confused.*

The bubbles appeared and then disappeared again before another message came through.

Rachel: *I really am sorry. I was a jerk.*

Blair: *You kinda were. So where do we go from here?*

Rachel: *Let me apologize properly. Dinner at my place?*

They would probably have sex after dinner. She tapped the phone with her thumb as she contemplated what she wanted from whatever this was—remembered the heat between them in Vegas—she wanted her.

Blair: *When?*

Rachel: *Tonight, if you're available.*

Blair: *Can't tonight. How about Sunday?* She was scheduled to do a wedding this evening.

Rachel: *That works for me. Say around six?*

Blair: *Okay. I'll see you then.* She quickly typed in *Wait. I don't have your address.*

Rachel sent her address, and she immediately copied and pasted it into the maps application on her phone to see where it was located. Hmm. Rachel lived in one of the nicer areas in Tampa. Only a thirty-minute drive from her house.

The door to her bedroom pushed open, and Morgan appeared with two cups of coffee. "You up?"

She dropped her phone to her side. "Yep." She sat up and leaned against the fabric headboard.

"Thanks for letting me crash here." Morgan entered the room and handed her a cup. "That was a surprise last night."

"Yeah. Everything went better than I expected. Not a single drunk in the crowd." She sipped her coffee and let its warmth fill her.

"The Friday events are pretty calm for the most part. But I'm talking about the woman." Morgan raised her eyebrows. "The one you met in Vegas." She was very perceptive.

"Oh, her. That *was* unexpected."

"Especially the way she ignored you."

"It was only a weekend fling. Don't read more into it than it deserves." She didn't intend to spill her feelings to Morgan.

"I did some recon and found out a little about her."

Blair scooted over and patted the side of the bed. "Well, don't keep me in suspense."

Morgan grinned and slid onto the bed next to her, leaning against the headboard as well. "Rachel was Shay's physical therapist. Shay had a bad accident last year and was in a coma for a while. She almost didn't make it."

"That's horrible."

"And that's not the half of it. Seems Shay and her wife, Chloe, were separated. The accident happened after they'd had an argument, and when Shay came out of the coma, she didn't remember they'd split. She'd lost close to a year of her memory."

"Wow. That's wild."

Morgan shifted toward her and raised her eyebrows. "I know. Right?"

"I guess it makes sense that they'd be close."

"I also found out that your friend Rachel took a quite shine to Shay and made it clear to Chloe that she'd be right there to step in if things didn't work out between her and Shay."

That's why she got the snub. "She's still hung up on her." She'd figured that out already.

"Looks like it. Admitting she had a wild weekend affair with you would let Shay know she was moving on." Morgan sipped her coffee.

She ignored the wild-weekend comment. Morgan was fishing. She hadn't elaborated on anything about what had happened between them. That just wasn't her style. "So, Rachel hasn't dated anyone since then?"

"Not from what I heard."

"Huh." No wonder she was so easy to please. Memories of Rachel mid-orgasm flashed through her mind. And so very vocal. "Then I guess it's good she didn't recognize me."

"You really think she didn't?"

"I have no idea, but I don't need that train wreck in my life right now." She didn't, but she was going to get on the rails with it anyway—even if it was only to the next stop. The sex was too hot to pass up. "You going to work the wedding with me tonight?" Morgan had already committed to it, but she needed a subject change.

"Absolutely. Can't pass up wedding tips." Morgan grinned.

"Okay. The wedding is at four, and the reception starts at five. So, we need to be there by three thirty to set up. You riding with me?"

"Yeah. It's supposed to rain later, so the motorcycle's out."

She'd bid this job a little cheaper than usual. The bride and groom had mentioned they had contacted Cocktail City, her main competition in the area that she'd hoped to pull business from in the future. This couple had plenty of friends, and their wedding would get her great exposure. Even so, she hoped the day went quickly because she couldn't wait to get to tomorrow to spend time with Rachel.

Blair tapped the keg and pumped it a few times before squirting the excess foam into a glass and dumping it into the trash can. She filled and emptied the glass several more times before she was satisfied it was ready to pour. Morgan had arrived early to help her fill the surrounding container with ice and chill the wine and champagne separately. They had all the essential soft drinks, along with the specifics for the specialty ones. Cups were different sizes and shapes for different beverages, as usual.

Soon the reception was in full swing. The food had been served, and most of the guests were seated and eating. A lot of people were here, and Blair was relieved to have a minute to breathe. Thankfully, it was an open bar, so she didn't have to do any math, make change, or keep track of tabs. Events with cash bars were difficult when they were busy. Tonight, the venue had supplied the alcohol, along with the wedding package. They had mostly served beer, wine, and basic two-ingredient cocktails. They'd had three or four half-hour-long bursts of being slammed and would have lots of downtime when the cake was cut and during toasts. As usual, they used that opportunity to restock the bar from the alcohol supplied by the venue.

The venue had three bar stations, two inside and one out on the terrace. She'd had to hire a few temps to help manage them, and they could've used a fourth. They'd been super busy, which was good and bad. Good that she hadn't had much time to think about Rachel, bad that her neck was starting to hurt. She really needed to get some shoes that provided more support. She'd looked a few times but found them all to be more masculine than she liked. She needed to get over that attitude and just buy a pair. She glanced up to see a pretty blonde zooming toward the bar.

"Hey. What's your name?" The blonde stood in front of Morgan, appearing impatient.

Don't tell her. Deflect and ask her name. Blair frowned.

"Mine?" Morgan looked up at the woman, and she nodded. "Morgan."

"What?" The woman leaned closer. This wedding had a live band, and it was excruciatingly loud.

"My name is Morgan."

She'd told Morgan a thousand times not to get friendly at weddings. It wasn't unusual for guests to hit on bartenders, and she didn't recommend giving out personal details.

"Hey, Morgan. Can you hook my table up with drinks tonight and keep them coming?"

"Sure. Just let your server know, and I'll send whatever you need."

"Thanks. You're a gem." The woman winked and smiled as she turned and stumbled back to her table.

"This wedding doesn't have drink servers except for the champagne toast."

"I know, but if I told her that, her next request would be that I deliver them, and that's not gonna happen." Morgan glanced at the table of mid-twenties guests. "Didn't see her drop anything into the tip jar either."

"You don't have to rely on tips. You're getting paid enough to do this." Blair had found some extra money in the budget to pay Morgan more than she'd originally planned.

"I know, but it's just the point. She asks for special service and thinks that her drunken smile will get it for her." Morgan poured a glass of wine for the woman in front of her. "If she keeps up this pace, I'm going to cut her off in about an hour."

"I think she's the sister of the groom, so let's give him a heads-up before you do that."

"Okay. You're the boss."

About twenty minutes later, the pretty blonde showed up again, screaming Morgan's name. "I thought you were going to hook me up?"

"Oh, yeah. Sorry about that. It seems the servers were only here for dinner, not for the bar."

"Well, then you bring the drinks."

"Sorry. I can't do that." Morgan glanced at Blair. "It's not in our contract."

"That's ridiculous. I put a fifty in your tip jar."

Morgan put her hand in the jar and swirled around the bills. "I don't see it." Bad move.

"What?" The woman became enraged and looked around the room. "I can't believe someone stole my tip from the jar."

Blair hadn't seen a bill larger than a five in the jar all night. She switched places with Morgan. "My liability insurance doesn't cover serving anywhere but at the bar." She glanced around the room to try to spot the groom. She wanted him close when she cut the blonde off. She wasn't going to take it well.

"We'll just see about that. I'm going to get my brother, and he'll straighten all this out."

"Thanks. I'll be happy to speak to him." That would save her a few steps. She only hoped he wasn't loaded as well. Another person from the blonde's table stood at the end of the bar and shouted Morgan's name.

"Seems to be your night." She grinned as Morgan rolled her eyes.

"What can I do for you?" Morgan was nothing if not polite, even in situations where the customer was belligerent.

"I need some water."

"Look down." She pointed to the brown water cooler on the table next to the bar.

"What?" The girl scrunched her eyebrows.

Morgan was busy making a couple of drinks, so Blair rounded the end of the bar and filled a glass from the water station. "Here you go." She handed it to her.

"Oh, wow." The girl seemed surprised. "Thanks. I didn't even see that."

She patted the cooler. "It's right here if you need more." Sometimes it was amazing how different one guest could be from the other.

She spotted the groom racing across the room, and he didn't look happy. Just what she needed.

He waved her over. "Sorry about my sister. She gets obnoxious when she's drunk."

She saw that. "Is she okay?"

"In the bathroom puking."

"I'm sorry. I didn't realize."

"Not your fault. She started early today." He took an envelope out of his pocket and handed it to her. "In case I don't get back here later. You guys have been awesome."

"Thank you." She hadn't expected a tip, and it felt thick. Cash that she'd split with Morgan.

She glanced at Morgan as he spun around and headed back to his bride. At least someone had manners. She slipped the money into her bag until she could deal with it later.

As the crowd dwindled, she started cleaning up. The reception had started at five, so it was still early, only a little after ten o'clock. They would shut the whole place down at eleven. The bride and groom had left hours ago. Was Rachel still up? Should she send her a text begging her to let her come by tonight? She massaged the kink in her neck and performed the exercise Rachel had shown her, remembering how she'd made it vanish so easily with the massage gun she'd left.

But she was tired and needed to rest up for whatever happened between them tomorrow night. The thought of that encounter sent a burst of energy through her. She plucked her phone from her back pocket and began texting Rachel. Waiting until tomorrow to see her would be torture.

CHAPTER SEVENTEEN

Two hours after Rachel had received the text from Blair, the doorbell rang, and she rushed to the door. She hadn't realized just how much she'd wanted to see Blair again until she'd kissed her Friday night. Was it bad to be so available? She pulled open the door and was immediately on fire. She didn't know if it was excitement or anxiety, but every one of her nerve endings was buzzing. Dressed in high-waisted skinny jeans and a white, loose-fitting, long-sleeved crop top, Blair stood on the porch facing the street, her mid-length auburn curls loose across her back. Rachel's system immediately went into overdrive. She was amazed at the impact Blair had on her.

"Hi." She almost couldn't get the two-letter word out.

Blair swung around slowly. "Hi." Her lush full lips slipped into a smile. "Nice neighborhood."

"It's okay." She moved out of the doorway and motioned Blair to come inside. "My neighbors are nice, and the yards are well groomed." What the hell? Was she a realtor all of a sudden trying to sell her a house?

"I see that." Blair stepped inside, dropped her bag on the closest piece of furniture, then turned around and pulled her into a scorching kiss that lasted a moment less than she'd wanted. "Sorry. I've been thinking about doing that all day."

"Me too." Rachel was about to explode. "I'm glad you were able to come tonight." She glanced at the kitchen. "Are you hungry?" She didn't have much, had planned to shop in the morning for tomorrow night's dinner.

Blair pulled her into her arms again. "Why don't we skip all the awkwardness and get down to why I'm here?"

"Fine by me." Rachel took her hand and tugged her into the bedroom.

She couldn't keep her hands to herself, and Blair seemed to be having the same issue as they battled for control. She wanted so badly to feel the way she had in Las Vegas. Until then she'd forgotten how good it was to be touched—to be wanted by another woman.

They fell onto the bed and synced like she did with no other. Blair knew all the right places and did all the right things to those places. It was amazing what she'd learned about her in one weekend.

When Rachel woke in the morning, Blair was gone. She flopped back into the pillow, disappointed that Blair had left without waking her. She shouldn't be. Last night, they'd agreed to keep it casual—no commitments—only sex—glorious sex. They'd spent hours making love to each other last night, but she'd thought they would have one more round before Blair left. A good-bye kiss would've been nice. She reached for her phone and found a note that Blair had laid on the nightstand.

Text me if you still want to do dinner tonight. You don't have to cook...we can just continue this, if you want.

She quickly texted Blair. *I definitely want to continue...and I want to make you dinner.* She punctuated it with a smiley face.

An immediate response came back. *I'll be there at six sharp.*

After reading the text she dropped her phone to the bed. She needed to talk this new arrangement through with someone but had no idea who to confide in. She and her mom were close, but she couldn't discuss her wild sexcapades with her. She could imagine the horror on her mother's face as she went through the whole no-strings scenario.

She didn't have any close friends, except for possibly Amy, but she was with her family on weekends, and Rachel absolutely wouldn't talk about her personal business with anyone else at work. That would be a career killer for sure. Discussing this situation with Shay was out of the question, even though she was positive Chloe had probably already told her. Perhaps Chloe was a possibility. She'd been so understanding before, but they weren't the closest of friends.

Their only real connection was Shay, but Chloe had accepted their friendship, which was more than she would've done after the confrontations they'd had during Shay's recovery. Still, it felt awkward to talk to her, or maybe Chloe had gotten past it all, and Rachel was the only one being weird about it—weird about everything.

Only one way to find out. She picked up her phone and typed in a text to Chloe. *Can we meet later to talk?*

She hadn't expected the bubbles on the screen to appear so quickly. Soon a message from Chloe popped up. *I'll be at the gallery later. Bring me lunch?* She wasn't weird about it at all.

Sure. See you then. She glanced at the time on her phone, almost eleven. She'd slept most of the morning away. The gallery opened at noon, and she would make it there by twelve thirty, so she wouldn't look quite so anxious.

Rachel pulled up to the menu board at the drive-through of her favorite sandwich shop and stared at the menu, trying to figure out what Chloe would like. She'd been here plenty of times with Shay, but never with Chloe. She vaguely remembered her liking all the usual condiments.

"Order when you're ready." The voice startled her when it blared through the speaker.

"Can I get a turkey and avocado on sourdough and an Italian on a roll?" She took a wild guess at the two most common sandwiches and figured she'd eat whichever one Chloe didn't pick.

"Sure. Do you want chips or cookies with those?"

"Chips, please." Always chips.

She pulled up and paid for the sandwiches and then took the short, ten-minute drive to the arts district.

The gallery looked empty as Rachel passed the plate-glass window to the door. "Hello," she sang as she entered.

"Back here." Chloe's voice rang through the gallery.

She made her way to the rear and down the step into the office space Chloe had created from the small room. "You shouldn't be back here when no one else is here with you."

"There's a bell." She glanced up at the small monitor on the shelf, touched the power button, and the screen came to life. "And cameras everywhere."

"You didn't even come out front to see who it was." She probably didn't keep the monitor on all the time either.

"I knew you were coming." Chloe relaxed into her chair. "What'd you bring me?"

She removed the sandwiches she'd picked up out of the bag. "Turkey and avocado or Italian?"

"Either one's fine." Who knew Chloe could be so accommodating?

"You want something to drink?"

"Coke, if you have it." She sat at the small, round table located strategically in the corner so someone could relax and keep an eye on the gallery through the opening to the front. "How about we split them both?"

Chloe set the sodas on the table and took a seat. "On second thought, I'll take the turkey." There she was—the decisive Chloe she was accustomed to. "Did you get pickles?"

"Of course." She ripped through the tape of the paper wrapping them and unrolled it, revealing the spears.

Chloe grabbed a bag of chips and tore open the top. "I need to have you bring me lunch more often. I don't get near the extras when Shay does it."

"She can't go to any restaurant without changing the standard meal."

"Right? And if they get it wrong, be prepared to send it back." Chloe bit her sandwich and chewed.

THE PROBABILITY OF LOVE

"Absolutely." They seemed to be bonding over weird-things Shay. "And whatever you do, don't start eating without her."

Chloe held her hand in front of her mouth as she laughed and chewed. "That would annoy most women, but it's one of the things I've learned to adore about her."

"I'm not sure I could've gone back to her like you did." She didn't quite understand their situation, but after watching Shay and Chloe interact at times, she wanted someone to want her that way.

"Believe me, a whole lot of soul-searching was involved in my decision." Chloe sipped her soda. "But in the end, she's the one for me." She bit of the end of a pickle spear, chewed, and swallowed. "Are you going to tell me why you're here, or do I have to drag it out of you?" She took another bite of her sandwich.

"You don't beat around the bush."

Chloe shook her head. "Well, we're not really *friends*. I mean, we both love Shay, but that's been the extent of it, until recently."

"True, and again, I'm sorry for everything I said to you when Shay was in the hospital."

Chloe held up her hand, found a napkin, and wiped her mouth. "We're way past that. Now spill."

Rachel unwrapped her sandwich. "You remember I told you about the woman I met in Las Vegas?"

Chloe raised her eyebrows. "The wild weekend affair?"

She nodded. Last night wasn't any less wild. "She's here." She nibbled at her sandwich.

"In Tampa?" Chloe dropped hers. "No way. How did you find her?"

"I didn't. You found her for me."

"What do you mean?" Chloe scrunched her eyebrows together.

"I ran into her Friday night. She's your new bartending service."

"Seriously? Wow." Chloe widened her eyes. "But you acted like you'd never met her before."

Heat burned the back of her neck, just as it had that night. "I was an ass—didn't know what to do, how to react. I never expected to see her again."

"I guess she was okay with that?" Chloe stood, went to the desk, and picked up a postcard.

"No. I went back later and apologized. She was gracious enough to accept my explanation." Rachel opened her soda and took a swig.

"Good move." Chloe brought the postcard back to the table. "I got this from Tess, our new artist, who recommended Blair. She's an awesome bartender, seems pretty smart and business savvy. She's also hot." She dropped it between them.

A tingle shot through Rachel when the picture of Blair in her form-fitting black pants and blouse came into view. *Definitely hot.* "I spent the night with her last night."

"And?"

"And it was a magnificent reminder of that weekend in Vegas."

"Do you plan to see her again?"

"Yes. Tonight. She's coming over for dinner." Rachel picked at her sandwich, too nervous to eat.

"Jumping right into it." Chloe grinned.

"We decided to get to know each other a little better but just keep it casual."

"Maybe it'll change into something more?"

"I doubt it. She works a lot of odd hours. Not really conducive to my schedule." Rachel wiped her hands on a napkin and picked up a pickle spear.

"I wouldn't rule it out just yet. I mean you just found out she's here, right?" Chloe wadded up her sandwich wrapper and tossed it into the trash. "Either way, good for you. You're having great sex, right?"

"Right." Was Chloe excited for her or just happy to know her competition for Shay was moving on? She finished half her sandwich and wrapped the rest up for later.

"So why aren't you telling all this to Shay?"

"You know why."

"Well, she's going to find out sooner or later."

"I figured you'd already told her about my weekend."

"I've thought about it more than once since you confided in me, but I try to avoid discussions with Shay about you when I can. I don't see you as a threat any longer, and Shay knows that. I don't want her to think that's changed." She cleaned up the rest of the remnants from lunch. "I can, if you want, but I think it would be better coming from you."

"You're probably right. I don't want to put you in a bad spot, but I might need a little time to figure it all out."

"I'm sure Shay will be happy to hear about Blair. You know she only wants the best for you. We both do."

She knew that, or Chloe would've thrown her out of their lives long ago for the way she'd acted during Shay's recovery. Her attitude had been totally uncalled for and unprofessional as well.

CHAPTER EIGHTEEN

B lair pulled up in front of the small, white, historic house. The drive wasn't long, since Rachel lived just north of Ybor City. She checked her makeup before she got out of the car and reached in the backseat for the six-pack of Corona she'd brought. She walked the pathway to the two steps that led to a massive gray, slat-floored porch. Two double-paned windows flanked each side of the front door. She turned and glanced back toward the street lined with palm trees and scattered weeping willows—a delightful view from any room in the house. She hadn't noticed any of that last night because she'd been on a mission. She moved forward and rang the doorbell.

The door opened almost immediately, and the vision before her was stunning. Rachel was dressed in long, flowy, tan pants and a tropical short-sleeve shirt. "Hi."

"Hi." Rachel smiled, and they stared at each other for a moment. "Come in." She motioned Blair through the entryway.

To her right was an office that contained a large wooden desk with two monitors, and to the left was a contemporary living area decorated in neutral tones. A rustic, brown coffee table separated two small beige couches to create a lovely social spot in front of a brick fireplace. She noted the large flat-screen TV above the fireplace—the perfect place to snuggle up and binge-watch on a rainy day. This was all new to her as well. She'd been focused on only one thing last night. In her defense, it had been dark and late.

She held up the six-pack. "I didn't know what to bring, but I know you like this."

"That was totally unnecessary, but thank you." Rachel took the beer from her and led her farther inside.

As she followed Rachel, the scent of something divine filled her nose. "What are you cooking?"

"So far, just rice with thyme in chicken broth." Rachel raised her eyebrows. "You're not vegan, are you?"

"Absolutely not." Blair grinned as she glanced around the room. "I think the burgers we scarfed down together in Vegas proved that." She dropped her purse next to the couch as she followed Rachel into the kitchen. It was elegantly modern, redesigned with multi-toned gray, slate tile, stainless-steel appliances, huge wooden cabinets, and gorgeous granite countertops.

"Oh yeah. I forgot about those." Rachel laughed. "I was so hungry I would've chewed my hand off if we'd waited much longer to eat."

"We found much better uses for your hands than that." She watched Rachel blush.

"Can I get you something to drink? A beer or a glass of wine?" Rachel tucked the beer away in the refrigerator and held the door open while she waited for Blair to answer.

Blair noted the open bottle of white wine on the counter. "Wine would be good." The dining room table was set nicely, complete with a white tablecloth, lit candles, and cloth napkins. The small bouquet of daisies in the middle set it off perfectly.

Rachel retrieved a glass from the cabinet, filled it halfway with wine, and handed it to her. Was Rachel afraid to get her drunk?

"Thank you." She put the glass to her lips and let the buttery flavor of the oak-aged chardonnay fill her mouth. "This is lovely."

"I can't take credit for choosing it. I'm not really a wine connoisseur, so I asked the woman at the liquor store to help me pick it out."

"Seems you asked the right woman." Blair moved closer and kissed Rachel gently on the lips. She'd been wanting to do that since she walked in. "Hi." She'd already said that, hadn't she?

"Hi." Rachel glanced between her eyes and her lips. "I'm glad you came." She slipped her arms around her waist and deepened the kiss.

"You need to stop that, or this wonderful dinner you've prepared is going to be left to get cold." Each time she got closer, she wanted Rachel more. "I can't be faulted for that."

"No." Rachel released her and went to the stove. "We are definitely eating first tonight." She dropped the sea scallops into a searing-hot pan and a moment later seemed to panic as she tried to lift one and it wouldn't break loose. "Oh, my gosh. These aren't turning out the way I planned." She finally pried the scallop from the pan and flipped it. "Why in the world did I choose scallops?"

"Calm down." Blair crossed the kitchen to the stove. "It'll be fine." She didn't cook scallops often. They were so delicious, yet so easy to ruin if you didn't have the timing right.

"I'm not much of a cook," Rachel said. "I eat at the hospital a lot. I'd originally planned on almond-crusted tilapia, but then I realized you could be allergic to nuts."

"I'm not allergic." Blair gently took the spatula from Rachel's hand and flipped the rest of the scallops. "Why don't you plate the rice?" She waited a minute and removed the scallops from the pan, splitting them between the two plates. "Look. They're perfectly seared." The pan sizzled as she poured a dash of white wine into it. "I need butter."

Rachel spun around, found the butter, and brought it to her. She cut a few pads, dropped them into the pan, and scraped the drippings free as she stirred.

"You really know what you're doing." Rachel watched Blair with amazement.

Blair drizzled the mixture over the scallops and rice. "I love to cook, just don't like doing it alone." Recipes never turned out the same when cooking for one.

"I'm more than happy to keep you company anytime you want my help, feeble as it may be." Rachel carried the plates to the table and slid into a chair.

Was that an open invitation? "I'll keep that in mind." Blair followed her and sat across from her.

Rachel closed her eyes and moaned as she chewed a bite. Blair stared at her intently, analyzing every freckle, every crease in Rachel's face. She was absolutely captivating.

Rachel's eyes popped open. "These are perfect. How did you do that?"

Blair cleared her throat—calmed the butterflies taking flight in her belly. "It just takes patience. You can't jiggle the pan or move the scallops around. You have to let them cook until you see caramelization reach the bottom edge." She scooped up a bite of scallop, along with some rice. The sweet, salty flavor of the sea filled her mouth. They were delicious.

"You don't have to pick one up to check?"

She shook her head. "Once you begin to see browning, leave the scallop alone for about twenty seconds. Count in your head or out loud if you have to. Then, you either flip it and move the pan to the oven or do what I did and flip it, pull it off the burner, and let the residual heat finish the job."

"Didn't know I was in the presence of an expert chef." Rachel grinned, and Blair's stomach tingled.

"Not even close, but I do know some of the basics." Blair had become friendly with a chef or two in Vegas who had given her some tips. "Did you remodel this house yourself?" She drank her wine, enjoying the way it complemented the scallops. Rachel had bought a delightful pairing, whether she knew it or not.

"Yeah. A professional had to do some things—plumbing and electrical—but with a little help here and there, I did most everything else."

Help from who? "You've done a fantastic job. It's gorgeous." Everything was so pristine. It matched Rachel perfectly.

"Thanks. I've been working on it for a while." Rachel glanced at her plate. "My friend, Shay, has been helping me. You met her the other night."

"Right." The complicated crush—the one who had her heart. A pang of jealousy gripped Blair. She needed to lock that little green monster away right now. They'd agreed to keep this casual, and that was what she intended to do—especially considering the circumstances. "And Chloe, her wife, does she help as well?" She still wanted to know.

Rachel nodded and pointed her fork to the watercolor seascape on the wall. "She helped me decorate. That's her art."

"That was sweet of them." That news relieved the knot that had begun to form in Blair's stomach. At least Chloe was aware of her wife's interactions with Rachel. Some of them anyway.

They ate in silence for a while, apparently no longer able to muster up enough chitchat to get them through the meal. She glanced over to see that Rachel had finished the last of her scallops and had relaxed into her chair to drink her wine. The look of pure desire Rachel gave her almost made her choke. She set down her fork and wiped her mouth before picking up her wineglass, rolling it between her hands and putting her elbows on the table.

"What are you thinking?" Blair held the wineglass between her hands with such pressure, it could shatter any minute.

"So, it's clear that we have a lot of chemistry, and we're good at taking action on it." Rachel pulled her eyebrows together. "At least I thought so." Seemed Rachel's confidence was faltering.

Blair nodded and took a sip of wine. "I'd have to agree on that. I wouldn't be here if that wasn't the case."

Rachel pressed her lips tightly together as she set her glass on the table. "So, do we want to set some ground rules?"

"I guess we should." Blair relaxed into her chair as she tried not to get caught up in the memory of being taken so many times, in so many ways, the night before.

"I'm good with this arrangement as long as you don't want a piece of my heart," Rachel said.

"I can agree to that." Blair replayed their time together in her head. She could be satisfied with many other parts of Rachel. She didn't have time for anything complicated right now, and Rachel's attachment to Shay was nothing but that.

Rachel bit her lip, seemed nervous all of a sudden. "I don't want you to think this is something I do often...I mean I did...but I told you before that I don't sleep with random women with no strings. At least not without seeing some sort of something more in the future with them. Permanent or not." She looked away as though Blair's stare was burning her eyes. "What happened in Vegas was new for me."

Time seemed to stand still as Blair recaptured Rachel's gaze—watched her insecurities surface in the candlelight. She hadn't glimpsed *this* Rachel before now and felt an urgent need to comfort her—calm the doubts that seemed to be holding her hostage.

"I can't say that I'm experienced at this kind of arrangement either." Blair pushed away from the table, stood, and walked slowly toward Rachel. "So, what do you say we figure it out together." She lowered herself slowly onto Rachel's lap.

Rachel gripped her ass and pulled her closer. "I'd like that."

The gentle kiss that came next sent a zap of electricity through Blair that lit up all her senses. It deepened at the speed of light as tongues and hands came into play. She could seriously kiss this vulnerable, insecure Rachel forever. She knew what was next—beyond the kissing—but she wanted to savor this moment—keep the anticipation strong as long as she could—make it last until she couldn't stand to wait any longer.

Rachel broke the kiss and paved a wet, hot path down her neck, raked her fingers up her sides, pulled her shirt up and over her head. Rachel sucked in a ragged breath as she ran her gaze over Blair's bra-clad breasts. "You're so beautiful." Her fingers roamed her back with a feather-light touch as she found the clasp of her bra and popped it open, guided the straps slowly down her arms.

Blair felt totally vulnerable and on display as Rachel cupped each of her breasts—engulfed a nipple with her mouth and swirled around it with her tongue. Jesus, she was wet. She grabbed hold of Rachel's shoulders and shifted—moved on Rachel's legs as Rachel moved beneath her—the friction delicious. She was completely ready to do whatever Rachel asked of her.

Rachel found her mouth again, danced with her tongue as she worked her fingers under the edge of her pants—fought the spandex to get inside.

Blair broke the kiss. "We should move this somewhere else, or I'm going to come right here."

"I'm okay with that." Rachel pushed her fingers farther, stroked between her folds as she moved them in and out. Blair couldn't stop the sensation spiraling through her—didn't want to. She gripped the back of the chair and let Rachel work her magic—let the orgasm take her—and it did immediately. She whimpered as she collapsed against Rachel, let her hold her. Coming so quickly was new for her. She'd been ready hours ago, and the anticipation had gotten to her.

Rachel chuckled as Blair jumped with each aftershock her fingers produced. "That was unexpected."

She leaned back and stared into Rachel's eyes. "Really? I thought you had the evening all planned out." Not that she hadn't started the whole thing.

"I did, but my plans for you were going to happen after dinner. Not during."

"I'm glad your timing was flexible." Blair grabbed Rachel's face and kissed her long and deep before she stood and held out her hand. "Let's go finish what you started."

"I'm all for finishing." Rachel looked up at her, dark hair all mussed around her face, desire clear in her eyes as she took her hand.

Blair pulled her up, wrapped her arms around her, and they were locked in another wildly erotic kiss. "And for starting again." Blair tugged her toward the back of the house. She had no idea where the bedroom was, but she would find it one way or another.

CHAPTER NINETEEN

It had been weeks since Blair had begun this no-strings affair with Rachel, and she was enjoying their arrangement more with every moment they spent together. She'd just taken dinner out of the oven when she received a text from Rachel.

Can we reschedule tonight? I'm out with friends and might be late.

She stared at the fully cooked chicken on the counter and sighed before she messaged back. *Sure, but I'm booked the next few nights, so it will have to be next week.* Not an attempt to guilt her into coming over. Just the facts.

Okay came through next.

Really? Was that it? No apology or anything? She was irritated at the short notice, irritated at herself for feeling that way. She hadn't told Rachel she was cooking, so she couldn't blame her for that reaction. But she was still upset.

They'd been getting together for weeks without any commitment. Why had that changed for her now? Why had she fixed an elaborate dinner without even telling Rachel? She'd wanted to surprise her—make her happy—enjoy the feeling that rushed her when she saw Rachel's reaction. What the fuck was she doing?

The drawer clanged as she jerked it open and grabbed the foil. She rolled out several large pieces before she stabbed the chicken and sliced the meat from its bones. The foil clattered with every piece she tossed onto it. She eventually abandoned the knife and tore into the carcass with her hands.

After cleaning up the massacre, she flopped onto the couch and thumbed through her schedule. The rest of her week *was* booked. Thursday, her second job at The Speak Easy. Friday, a birthday party. Saturday, another wedding. Sunday, a ladies' club brunch. Rachel wasn't coming over tonight, and it would be days before she would see her again. She breathed deeply to settle her disappointment. Might as well work on her website. She had nothing else planned tonight.

The frustration built higher as she fiddled with the page changes and nothing looked the way it should. Why hadn't she created instructions for herself the last time Tess had shown her how to make them? More important, why hadn't she just taken Tess up on her offer to handle the changes for her? What took Blair an hour to get right would take Tess only five minutes. She picked up the phone and called her.

Tess's bright, cheerful, voice came through the speaker. "Hey. What's up?"

"I'm working on my website, and every time I make a change, it looks all wonky. I can't get it to look the way I want it to."

"Wonky, huh?" Tess giggled. "Why don't you just send me the changes, and I'll update it tomorrow."

"I want to do it tonight. I have nothing better going on."

"Uh-oh. That doesn't sound right. Where's Rachel?"

"I made dinner for her, and she cancelled on me. She's out with *friends*." She could hear the irritation in her voice and was disappointed in herself.

"You made dinner for her? I thought you two were keeping it casual."

"Can't people have dinner together and still be casual?"

"Sure. But it sounds like you're upset that she didn't show."

"I know—I am. I shouldn't be. I didn't tell her I was cooking."

"Ohhhh." Tess was evidently getting the picture now. "It's not casual for you anymore, is it?"

"I don't think so. I've been trying my best to keep it that way, but I'm in way over my head here, Tess."

"Does she know? Have you talked to her about it?"

"No. I can't. We agreed to no strings, and she's clearly not feeling the same about the arrangement."

"Are you in love with her?"

"I wouldn't go that far, but I definitely care about her." She was certainly moving in that direction.

"Nothing wrong with that. Friends care about each other, Blair."

"I need to figure out how to keep my feelings at the friendship level." That would be impossible. She'd blown past the friend stage weeks ago.

"Doesn't sound like you're going to be able to do that. You need to tell her how you feel. I know you made an agreement and are unsure of what might happen if you do, but let her know anyway."

"I'm not sure I can. I'm scared of how I feel, Tess. Absolutely terrified that she doesn't feel the same. What if she just walks away from me?"

"Well, then you'll know exactly how she feels." Tess's calm, even tone wasn't helping as it usually did. "You need to start being honest with yourself—and her. Listen. I have to go. Sophie's home, and she's brought sushi. You want to come over and eat? She always buys a ton. We can talk more...get Sophie's take on the situation."

"Thanks, but no. I'm going to stay home and wallow in my feelings." She wasn't up for having her emotions analyzed.

"Okay, but don't sink too low. And send me the changes for your website. I'll get them done tomorrow."

"I will. Thanks." She dropped her phone to the couch, closed her laptop, and grabbed the remote. TV would be her only companion tonight.

When she finished bingeing a few episodes of a show Rachel hadn't been interested in, she clicked off the TV, went to the bedroom, and crawled into bed.

She swept her arm across the bed and felt the cool emptiness of it. She'd gotten used to not being alone, used to having Rachel's soft body next to her with legs and arms wrapped everywhere. The warmth she provided when she rolled over and burrowed into her, Rachel's soft, rhythmic breathing in her ears, soothed her from the day's stress when she couldn't fully wind down.

Fuck. She'd done all this to herself.

❖

It was almost eleven, and Rachel was ready to be at home and in bed. She'd quit drinking a couple of hours ago because Amy hadn't been out in a while and was taking full advantage of the bar. A couple of other friends from work had joined them, but they'd left earlier, so it was just the two of them now. She glanced at her phone, scrolled through the text message she'd sent Blair earlier. She'd been short with her for her own survival. She'd needed this night out—needed to be away from Blair.

"Everything okay?" Amy grinned at her, glassy-eyed. Rachel would be the taxi driver tonight for sure.

She nodded. "Blair sounded upset when I cancelled."

"She was probably looking forward to a night of wild sex."

"Maybe so, but now I feel bad."

"Why's that?" Amy sipped her drink.

"We agreed to just sex, no commitments of any kind." What did that really mean?

"Yet you want more."

"I think I do. But I set the ground rules." Getting close to Blair made her uncertain about everything she'd planned for this arrangement to be. She wouldn't be in control any longer, and that scared the hell out of her.

"If you set them, you can change them. Right?"

"Maybe. She didn't object, so I think she wants to keep it casual too." But then why would she be upset if I didn't come over? Sexual frustration? She was feeling a bit of that herself right now.

"What about Shay?"

"What about her?" Rachel always knew what to expect from Shay—hope, but not commitment.

Amy moved closer, shouted into her ear, "Are you still secretly pining away for her?" Her volume was nowhere near a whisper.

"You, my dear, are drunk." She backed away, put a small bit of distance between them.

"Stop avoiding my question." Amy wasn't letting up.

"Shay's never going to leave Chloe. Her marriage is solid."

"You're letting her go." Amy's eyes widened, and her lips cracked into a huge smile. "Thank God you've finally realized that

fact about Shay. That woman has kept you prisoner long enough."
Amy knew all her secrets.

"I wouldn't say she's done that."

"I would. She calls you way too much, expects ridiculous things from you—things she should get from her wife."

"I don't mind doing them."

"You fucking should." Amy lurched forward in her chair. "She takes advantage of your feelings for her." She scrunched her eyebrows together. "It must be nice to have you, along with her wife, to keep her happy." Amy seemed to have an issue with Shay. Rachel hadn't been aware of that fact, but then again, she didn't go out drinking with Amy much.

"All right. Your filter's totally gone. It's time get you home." She took the glass from Amy's hand and set it on the table. "You still have kids to get up and off to school in the morning."

"Jason said he'd take care of that tomorrow." Amy swayed as she stood. "But my head will thank you for taking me home now."

Even though Amy worked the twelve-to-eight shift, which would give her time to recover, her head would be telling her she should've left before that last drink.

CHAPTER TWENTY

B lair went out to her van to get her shirt for the evening wedding event, but it wasn't hanging on the hook where she usually put it. "Fuck." She'd been in such a hurry to get to Rachel's last night, she must've left it on the couch. It had been days since she'd seen her. She was still working on tamping down her emotions, but she'd been able to push herself back into casual mode when Rachel had invited her over last night. It had been too many days since she'd been able to touch her. She rushed back inside and gathered her things.

"What's up?" Rachel watched her.

"I have to go home and get ready for tonight."

"I thought you brought your clothes with you."

"I thought I did too, but I can't find my shirt."

"Hang on." Rachel bolted from the couch. "I probably have one you can borrow."

"It's formal, so I need a white button-down. I don't suppose you have a bow tie to go with that?"

"I just might. You're talking to a soft butch who's attended a fancy event or two." She pushed open her closet, slid a few hangers apart, and took out a white dress shirt. "How about this one?" She slipped a couple of ties from the peg on the inside closet wall. "Black okay?"

"Perfect."

"Okay then." She spun and went to the door. "I'll be waiting for the fashion show in the living room."

Blair slipped on the shirt and checked herself in the full-length mirror on the back of the door. It was a little snug on her boobs but still fit well. She found her pants in her bag and slipped them on before she attempted to tie the bow tie. It wasn't perfect, but it would do for tonight. She headed out into the living room. "What do you think?"

"Hold on." Rachel got up from the couch, looked her dead in the eyes, and with a smile and a wink, tucked her shirt into her pants for her. "A little was hanging out there in front."

All her senses fired in the usual manner. "How do you do that?"

"What?"

"Turn me on so quickly."

"It's a gift." Rachel tugged at the bow tie and straightened it. "I kinda like the way my shirt fits you." She kissed her. "I can't wait to take it off you later."

"I'm probably going to be really late tonight. The event lasts until one. Maybe we should reschedule?"

"Oh. Okay." Rachel seemed disappointed. "Or I can just sleep at your place, and we can catch up on our shows in the morning."

"You could do that." She was surprised at how much she wanted that to happen—how happy it made her. Since their schedules differed so much, she'd given Rachel a key, so she could go over anytime. "We can have pancakes."

"And bacon?"

"Yes. Bacon. Extra crispy, the way you like it." She swept Rachel into her arms and kissed her before she grabbed her bag, went to the door, and pulled it open. "There's plenty of food in the fridge if you want to go over early."

"I might just do that." Rachel rushed over and gave her one last kiss good-bye before she left.

She glanced over her shoulder at Rachel standing in the doorway as she walked to her van. She could get used to this—in fact she was already used to it. How had she gotten so lucky? How had she gotten so careless with her feelings?

❖

Morgan was already at the venue when Blair arrived. She'd been unsure of her at first, but Morgan had proved to be a hard worker—always on time and always ready to go the extra mile to get the job done. She hadn't mentioned it to her, but she was considering bringing Morgan in as a partner sometime in the future, if she was interested.

This wedding called for two signature craft cocktails, the bride's choice as well the groom's, and all the other basics, plus champagne and beer. She hadn't been able to convince the couple to go with an easy big-batch cocktail. They'd had clear ideas about what they wanted. Thankfully she was able to bring them in line with what she could provide. The bride chose a ginger mojito, while the groom chose a slightly more complicated brown-butter old-fashioned. He couldn't decide which flavor he liked best, so she'd opted to provide several varieties of proof syrup, including pecan, black walnut, and orange for the non-nut lovers. The caterer was supplying the common garnishes such as maraschino cherries, olives, onions, and citrus. She'd sent them the types and quantities weeks ago. That left the dark cherries, bitters, and simple syrups to her.

She always planned on three drinks each for guests, but they usually drank more in warm-weather outdoor weddings. Blair watched Morgan tug at her collar. She had no idea why anyone would want to have an outdoor wedding in this heat.

"This humidity is something." She placed the garnishes within each of their sections in the flip-top container on the bar.

"Here they come." Morgan stood ready to serve.

The first of the guests had started to arrive—a slow trickle of people headed directly to the bar before finding their seats. Soon they would be slammed. Generally, after the ceremony, weddings had them pushing out thirty-plus drinks within the span of fifteen minutes to a half hour. With beer and wine that was easy, but factoring in the cocktails and the bride and groom's specialties made it a bit tricky.

Soon they were overwhelmed and had no time to think about what they were doing. Everything was routine—drink recipes ingrained in their heads from countless nights tending bar.

"Look at them." Morgan watched a few kids whirl around on the dance floor. "Having a great time. Free of all responsibilities."

"You having trouble at your day job?"

"Not trouble, really. I just don't know what I want to be when I grow up." Morgan refilled a couple of glasses of wine for the man in front of her. "How did you decide what you wanted to do and figure all this out? You seem to have it all together."

"It might seem that way now, but my first attempt at college was a disaster."

"Really?"

"Yeah. I did the whole general-studies thing my first year and hated it." Blair wiped down the bar. "I was waiting tables at night to afford living expenses and didn't have much time to study."

"I don't know why they make you take all those classes anyway. They have nothing to do with the career path."

"They want us to be well-rounded." She changed out the almost-empty container of limes with a fresh one. "I probably would've never found that I had a passion for writing if I hadn't taken them."

"Are you still writing?"

"Some. When the inspiration hits me." It had hit her hard since Rachel had appeared in her life again.

A twenty-something man approached the bar. "Can I get a rum and coke?"

"Sure." Blair hadn't recalled him ordering that earlier but could be mistaken. She handed him the drink and watched him walk to a table and immediately hand it to another guy, who looked much younger. "We're going to have to watch that one." Weddings were notorious for people passing drinks off to underage relatives.

"I know. He's not the only person he's supplying."

"Why don't these guys just bring a flask like they did in the old days?"

"That would mean they'd actually have to purchase the alcohol, and frat boy doesn't look to be well off." He was dressed in khaki pants and a blue plaid shirt, no tie. Not the expected attire for a formal wedding. "I wonder if he was even invited?"

Morgan's new customer interrupted her surveillance. "Can you juggle those bottles?"

"I can, but I won't." Morgan knew the limitations of the liability insurance.

"I bet you can't." The guy obviously thought he was cute, passive-aggressively flirting with Morgan. Apparently, her butch appearance didn't give him a clue that she was gay.

"Believe me, she can, but we don't do that at events." She switched places with Morgan. "You want to try the groom's special?"

"I think I'll have the bride's." He leaned closer. "Can you make that extra special for me?" A couple of women rushed up and stood next to him, and he turned his attention to them. "Hello, ladies. Can I buy you a drink?" They nodded, and he motioned for two more of the bride's special.

Apparently, any woman would do for this guy. Blair quickly made their drinks, and he followed them back to their table. Poor girls. She relaxed and watched the people on the dance floor as she enjoyed the lull in guests. "Watching drunk people dance is so entertaining."

Morgan nodded. "It makes me feel so much better about myself all around."

Blair scanned tables for possible drink refills to gauge the next rush. Frat boy and friends had abandoned their drinks for the dance floor. "I'll be right back." She wandered over and collected the half-empty glass of rum and coke, along with several empty glasses. That would be frat boy's last drink from the bar tonight. She glanced around the room and thought she spotted Paige from Cocktail City, her competition. Why the hell was she here? Blair dropped the glasses at the bussing stand, then immediately headed across the room. A guest crossed Blair's path and they collided. When she looked again, Paige was gone. Must've been her imagination.

The rest of the night went smoothly. She'd had to shut down frat boy rather quickly—threatened to cut him off entirely if he kept it up. That seemed to have worked. At least she hadn't seen him sharing in plain sight after that.

"Any plans for later?"

"Nope." Blair shook her head. "I don't know where you get your energy."

Morgan held up an energy drink. "Stamina in a can."

"Planning on staying up all night?"

"It's possible."

"Where do you go after these events?" Blair knew of a couple places open late, but they didn't seem like Morgan's style.

"Sometimes to an after-hours club, but tonight I'm going to a private party. Want to come along?"

"Thanks, but no. I'm going home and falling straight into bed." Into Rachel's areas in the bed. She was ready to be done—at home snuggled up in her comfort zone. The thought of taking that whole scenario into morning excited her.

Last call was always an issue, so she didn't advertise it loudly. Drunk and entitled guests didn't understand why they couldn't get more. She always found the location of a couple of nearby bars, or in this case, she'd send them to the hotel bar to continue the festivities. When the venue was at a small boutique hotel, that could be considered a douche move, but the hotel had a large bar and could handle them.

Blair picked up the tip jar and studied the contents. "Look at that. Uncle Bo left you a twenty."

"It pays to be nice." Morgan grinned. "This was a pretty good crowd."

"Other than frat boy, I would have to agree."

"Don't forget vodka-soda Sally." She'd come to the bar several times, had been very friendly, and had left them large tips.

"Oh, yeah. She was a treat. We need more Sallys in the world."

Once the bar was put up, Blair headed out. She couldn't wait to get home. A nice hot bath and a warm bed used to be the only reason she rushed home, but now she just wanted to slide into bed with Rachel.

CHAPTER TWENTY-ONE

Rachel didn't venture out much on weeknights, but tonight she was attending a new artist's opening at the gallery. She would've stayed home, but Blair was running the bar. She'd rather be escorting her, but that would be against the protocol they'd set for this arrangement of convenience. Did it really matter? They were already straddling the line they'd set for themselves. Months had gone by since they'd made the agreement, and they seemed to have settled into a routine that Rachel liked. Blair stayed mostly at Rachel's because it was closer to her second job at The Speak Easy, and she was usually out early in the mornings. She'd get home and fix something easy for dinner, or Blair would bring something later when she was done working. They were always up late or ridiculously early, which was becoming exhausting. She'd begun using her evenings when Blair was working to nap.

The company was good, and the sex hadn't changed—still off the charts. She only wished their schedules synced better. Most days Blair still worked at The Speak Easy, except on weekends, when she handled events like tonight for her own business, Blissful Bubbles.

It felt weird being across the room from Blair. She wanted to steal her away into the back room and ravage her. She'd already attempted, but Blair had resisted—said she didn't want to lose this gig, which was steady income that she needed to keep her business going. Rachel couldn't argue with that.

Chloe appeared beside her. "You seem to have settled into a routine with Blair." She was always fishing for more information.

"I guess I have." She watched Blair across the room pouring wine for Shay.

"What does that mean for you?" Chloe watched as well.

"I don't know." She really didn't at this point, only that she liked having Blair around.

"You can't go on being in love with Shay forever." Chloe smiled softly. "We're happy, and that's not going to change."

"I know you are, and I would never try to come between you." She veered her gaze from the bar to Chloe. "It's hard to move on when you thought you'd found—" Now that Blair was in her life, she honestly couldn't find the right word or even remember how she felt about Shay before. The feelings just weren't there any longer.

"Your soul mate?" Chloe lifted an eyebrow.

"Something like that. You know it was entirely unintended. I fell in love with a vulnerable, innocent woman, who ended up being not so innocent. By the time I found that out, it was too late."

Chloe pulled her eyebrows together. Seemed she might be taking exception to that statement about Shay's innocence. "We all make mistakes, and my love for her outweighed her mistake. That's why we're still together." Chloe gazed across the room at Shay. "Plus, she promised it would never happen again. After all we've been through, I believe her."

"I don't know if I could've been as forgiving as you were." She caught a glimpse of Blair when Shay left the bar, and her stomach tingled.

"I didn't either until I almost lost her." The trauma seemed to have solidified the bond between Chloe and Shay.

Shay handed Chloe a glass of wine. "What are you two talking so seriously about?"

"How gorgeous you look in that outfit." Chloe glanced at Rachel. "I did an excellent job of dressing her tonight, didn't I?"

"Hey. I picked the shirt." Shay plucked at the green, pastel button-down.

"That you did. It was a wonderful match." Chloe leaned closer and kissed Shay lightly on the lips.

Rachel didn't look away. Her stomach didn't tighten as it usually did. The affection between Shay and Chloe didn't seem to affect her now. She glanced at Blair, and when Blair smiled at her and winked, the constant burn in her belly flared. The hot flame she felt with Blair was soon going to burn through the thread of hope she'd had for Shay too long.

Rachel slipped out of bed and into the kitchen. She needed food. She put on a pot of coffee before opening the refrigerator and scanning the sparse contents. Blair usually had plenty of food. There wasn't any bacon, but she found eggs and a bag of grated cheddar cheese, opened it, and sniffed before she set it on the counter next to the stove. Then she reached back inside for the half-full jar of strawberry jam. She located a loaf of bread on the counter—a staple at Rachel's house, sent from the gods just for her. Seemed to be that way at Blair's as well. Scrambled eggs and toast it would be.

She opened a few drawers looking for a spatula and found a leather-bound journal instead. She picked it up, then put it back, closed the drawer, and kept hunting the spatula again, finally finding one. Once the eggs were scrambled and in the pan, she glanced at the drawer that contained the journal. It was a total invasion of privacy, but she wanted to know Blair's thoughts—what she'd written about her. She slid open the drawer and took out the journal. She'd learned things about Shay from her journals—deeply personal things she'd never expected. She could do the same with Blair. She tussled with that thought before she shoved the book back in the drawer and closed it. She stirred the egg as she glanced around the kitchen and widened her eyes when she spotted another leather-bound book in a stack of magazines close to the wall on the breakfast bar. She sprinted across the kitchen and fished it out of the pile. This one was in plain sight—not so much of a violation.

The first page contained several written paragraphs but wasn't dated. Maybe it wasn't a journal. She read the first section. They were verses—poetry of some kind.

My soul was empty, cold and still.
Like birds, singing sweet melodies,
Warmth soon flooded through,
Filling it with music again.

Was this about her or someone else? She flipped through the page and read another eloquent poem.

You've taken me to places deep inside your soul that you've kept hidden away for far too long, beautiful echoing emotions within you that show me who you truly are.

You, my love, are like an unfinished canvas. Every day is like a freshly made brushstroke, adding another vibrant layer of color to you, an incredibly remarkable work of art.

Tess was written at the bottom. Did Blair have a past with Tess?

"Are you cooking for me?" Blair's voice startled her.

"Yes." She dropped the book and pushed it back toward the stack of magazines and rushed to the stove again. "Trying, anyway. You didn't have as much stuff as usual in your refrigerator."

"I haven't had time to shop. Looks delicious." Blair brushed her back with her hand as she kissed her softly before she took a couple of pieces of bread from the bag and dropped them into the toaster. "You found my poetry book?"

"I did. I read a few pages. I hope you don't mind." She cringed.

"It's okay. I just picked it back up again. I hadn't written anything in a while." Blair reached for a couple of plates from the cabinet.

She needed to ask about Tess, clear it up now before she got in whatever this was with Blair any deeper. "I saw the one you wrote for Tess. Were you involved with her?"

"No." Blair shook her head. "Tess wrote that for Sophie. It's so romantic, isn't it?"

"Yes. Very." She scrunched her eyebrows together. "Why do you have it in your book?"

"Tess, Sophie, and I have a bit of history. Kind of a weird story." She picked up the jar in front of her. "Jam?"

She nodded. "I'm listening." She added eggs to each plate.

The toast popped up, and Blair grabbed the pieces and began slathering them with jam. "I met Sophie online, and we messaged each other some. I thought we had something, so I invited her to meet me for a weekend at a resort I used to work at. Sophie chickened out, and Tess showed up instead." She carried the plate of toast to the table before she went to the refrigerator. "Juice?"

"Yes. Please." Her gut twisted as she found the forks in one of the drawers she'd opened earlier. She didn't like the idea of anyone hurting Blair. "That sounds awful." She carried their plates to the table and sat waiting for Blair and the rest of the story.

"It wasn't great." Blair slipped into the chair adjacent from her. "But Tess came clean about the situation. She'd been helping Sophie communicate with me."

"Tess fell in love with you?"

Blair shook her head as she chewed. "She fell in love with Sophie and vice versa. I was an unwitting catalyst. They've been friends for a long time and didn't realize their feelings until I was in the middle. It was all pretty confusing until I figured it out."

"I'm not sure what to say." Only that she was glad it didn't work out, or Blair wouldn't be here with her now. She pushed her eggs around on her plate with her fork before capturing a small portion on it.

"I kinda saw it before they did. It was hard for them to admit." Blair bit into her toast.

"They seem like a great couple."

Blair took a sip of juice and swallowed. "They are. I think they were afraid it would ruin their friendship. Seems to have only made it stronger."

"It's nice that you remained friends with them."

"Tess was persistent. She felt bad and wouldn't let me alone."

"She's a good person." Rachel was relieved to hear there hadn't been anything romantic between Blair and Tess.

"I agree."

"Would you mind if I read more of your poetry?" The insight could be fascinating.

"No, but it's not all good."

"I'd have to disagree. What I've read so far has been lovely." She sipped her juice. "How long have you been writing?"

Blair tilted her head as she chewed, as though digging deep into her memory. "Probably since I was in my teens. It was a way to get my thoughts out of my head."

"Wow." She held up the book. "So you have plenty of these."

Blair nodded. "I have more somewhere around here, and some are boxed up in the attic at my parents' house." She laughed. "My dad keeps saying I'll have to take them all someday."

"Parents." She rolled her eyes. "Always complaining about storing things."

"Right?" Blair laughed along with her.

Breakfast with Blair was easy, just as the night before had been. They'd had sex only once during the night because Blair was tired. She'd seemed to want comfort more than anything else, and Rachel was okay with providing it.

Blair stood at the door to the hospital physical-therapy unit and watched Rachel work with a young girl, helping her as she attempted to walk between the parallel bars. Rachel stood in front facing her, her gaze focused on the girl's as she struggled to take a step. The girl took one step and then another before she fell into Rachel's arms and began to cry. Rachel held her tightly before she swept her up and carried her to the wheelchair sitting at the other end of the bars. The girl wasn't large, but still Blair was mesmerized by Rachel's strength, along with her gentleness. She suddenly had a new appreciation for Rachel and her work. It had to be so rewarding to help people gain their mobility—their lives back.

A voice interrupted her thoughts. "We don't allow spectators in the PT room. Can I help you with something?"

"Sorry. I'm here to see Rachel. I didn't want to disturb her while she was working with a patient."

"If you'll wait out in the hallway, I'll let her know you're here." The woman turned to go back inside. "Can I get your name?"

"Blair."

"Oh. So, you're free and easy?" The woman covered her mouth as her cheeks reddened. "I'm sorry. That sounded horrible."

"Um, I'm not exactly sure what to say to that." She wasn't lying. What she and Rachel had *was* free *and* easy. She just hadn't expected

THE PROBABILITY OF LOVE

that description from a total stranger. Maybe coming here wasn't such a good idea.

"I'm Amy." She held out her hand. "Rachel just mentioned that you and she meshed well."

It seemed that Rachel was talking about her—and it seemed to be all good. "Nice to meet you." She shook Amy's hand.

Amy held up a finger. "I'll go get her."

Rachel came through the door soon after Amy went inside. "Hey. This is a nice surprise." She smiled widely as she hurried to her. "What are you doing here? Shouldn't you be at work?"

"I'm on my way. I went by the deli and picked up a sandwich for later and got one for you as well." She handed her the bag. She'd wanted to see her again before her shift.

"Ooh. What kind?" The paper rustled as she opened it and peered inside.

"Turkey on wheat, mustard, mayo, lettuce, and tomato. Your favorite...I think."

"Absolutely." Rachel grinned and bit her lip before she kissed her softly. "I can't believe you remembered."

She remembered everything Rachel liked from the moment they'd met in Las Vegas.

"I guess the fried foods at the bar are getting to you?"

"Getting to my hips."

"Your hips are perfect." Rachel touched them softly. "As is the rest of you."

Rachel knew exactly what to say. Her stomach tingled as she moved closer and kissed her deeply. She wanted to sweep Rachel up into her arms and make the kiss last for hours. "As much as I would love to stand right here and kiss you forever, I can't. I'm already late for work."

"Okay. Let me set this inside and grab my jacket, and I'll walk you out." She spun and rushed away.

Blair should've brought a jacket herself. Rain was forecast for this afternoon, but she hoped it held off until she was already at the bar.

Rachel walked her out to the parking lot. They were halfway to her van when suddenly the wind came up, and the sky darkened. "Oh

• 149 •

my God. I'm going to get soaked before I can make it to the van." Blair panicked and started running.

Rachel grabbed her arm. "Wait." She immediately slipped off her rain jacket and helped Blair put it on, zipped it, and pulled the hood over her head. She tucked Blair's hair behind her ears. "There you go." Rachel laced their fingers together and continued to walk.

The sky opened up, and a deluge of rain covered them. By the time they reached the van Rachel was soaked, and all Blair could see was how sexy she was. Blair hit the clicker, and the doors unlocked. Rachel opened the door for Blair and then took her face in her hands and kissed her. In that moment that was all she cared about. It didn't matter that it was raining anymore. She didn't care about getting her clothes wet or even if the rain soaked through them to the bone.

The rain had slowed to a trickle by the time she climbed inside the van. "I can't believe you did that. Look at you. You're soaked."

"I have scrubs to change into inside." She turned toward the building.

"Wait. Get in, and I'll drop you at the door." She'd never had a woman do anything like that before, and her heart opened a little more.

Rachel ran around the van and climbed into the passenger seat. Blair grabbed a bar towel from the pile she kept in the van and handed it to her. "Not that this will help much." She held up the fifteen-by-eighteen terry cloth. "But I have a dozen more in the back if you need them."

The laughter that flew from Rachel's mouth was contagious. She snatched the towel from her and blotted her face. "It's surprisingly absorbent."

"They're lint-free as well." She grinned.

"I'm going to keep this for now." Rachel jerked her lip to one side. "I'll keep it safe under my pillow until you come looking for it tonight."

A bolt of electricity flew through Blair. Rachel could have everything she possessed for another look like that.

She fired the engine and dropped Rachel at the door, then waited and watched as she got out of the car and walked to the entrance. The rain didn't seem to bother her at all. It would've totally ruined

Blair's evening if Rachel hadn't given up her jacket to keep her dry. Her stomach tingled when Rachel turned and gave her a wave before she walked inside. *Is this what being addicted to something feels like?* Blair had seen addiction a lot while working as a bartender, but she'd never experienced it.

Sleepovers were becoming a necessity with the hours Blair worked, and she was getting used to having Rachel around all the time. Rachel was everything she'd hoped for in a companion—sweet, fun, and gorgeous. Most nights they spent at Rachel's place, except for when Blair worked late, and then she'd come home to find Rachel in her bed, semiconscious, waiting for her.

She'd even tried to beg off for a few days during her period because sometimes it hit her so hard she didn't want to have sex and could be very unsociable. Rachel had told her that didn't bother her either way and had shown up anyway with microwave popcorn and sodas to just hang out and watch TV. As time went on, some nights were filled with sex, others just sleep. Their arrangement was becoming more than convenience for her—more than either of them had planned, which wasn't good since Rachel had been the one to set the no-strings boundaries. Plus, Rachel still maintained a lot of contact with Shay while Blair was working.

CHAPTER TWENTY-TWO

The phone rang, bringing Rachel out of her sleep. It had been a late night again last night, and not wanting to disturb Blair, she stretched to reach it on the nightstand. It was her mother, which meant she had to answer, or she'd just keep calling.

"Hi, Mom," she said softly.

"Hi, honey. You sound groggy. Did I wake you?"

"No. I'm awake. Just nursing a headache."

"Oh. Did you take something for it?"

"Yes." She hadn't, because she didn't really have a headache. Just didn't know how else to explain her raspy voice. She couldn't very well tell her mother that she didn't want to wake the woman who'd made her come several times during the night. Screaming during orgasms was getting to be a habit she didn't want to give up.

"I'm cooking dinner tonight. Your brother's coming, and he's bringing the kids."

"Without Lori?" Why in the world would Ben come without her?

"She's got some candle party planned, and he needs to get out of the house. She might be over later. Didn't you get the invitation to her party?"

"I did, but I forgot about it." She hated those parties because she always felt pressured to buy more than she needed. "I'll get a couple from her separately."

"Good, because she's really trying to make a go of this business. Ben said it's given her something to do outside of taking care of the kids. Really changed her in a good way."

"That's nice to hear." Lori had been struggling with the stay-at-home-mom role since all their kids started going to school. "I'm glad she's found something she likes to do." No way could Rachel give up her career permanently to stay home and take care of the kids. She glanced at Blair, still asleep in the crook of her arm. Did Blair feel that way too? Did she even want kids? Why was she even considering that question, thinking about this subject at all?

Her mom interrupted her spiraling thoughts. "Dinner's at six. Bring wine."

"Got it. See you then. Love you." She waited for the usual "I love you" back and hit the end button.

Blair leaned her head back and looked at her, emerald-green eyes staring up at her in question.

She almost couldn't speak. What was happening to her? "My mom." She bounced her head from side to side. She shouldn't invite Blair to dinner. That move would definitely promote her from casual to something more. "She's cooking dinner tonight. You wanna go?" Too late. Her heart took the lead before her brain kicked in.

"I'd love to." Blair snuggled closer, Rachel immediately enveloping her in warmth.

"When you got home last night, I forgot to ask you how your shift went. It's hard to focus on anything else when you take off your clothes and crawl into bed."

"That goes both ways."

"So how was it?"

"Forget about last night. I have work to do right now." Blair crawled down her and buried herself between her legs.

As she clutched the sheet and felt the first swipe of Blair's tongue, she couldn't agree more with her priorities.

Rachel pulled up in front of her parents' house and put the car in park. She'd let her mom know she was bringing a guest. That was probably why her brother's SUV was already in the driveway. She'd hoped to beat him there so she could give Blair a sort of tiered introduction—first her parents, and then her brother, with a little breather in between. She gripped the gear shift. Maybe this wasn't such a good idea after all. She'd filled Blair in on her father's direct demeanor, and she seemed to be okay with discussing anything and everything if it came up.

"Are you okay?" Blair covered her hand on the gear shift.

"I'm fine. Why?"

"You haven't said a word since we got into the car, and you're about to pull the shifter out of the console."

It wasn't a long drive, only about fifteen minutes, but Blair was right. She'd been wrapped up in her own thoughts about how the night could play out. She was nervous and had no idea why this visit was paralyzing her this way.

She let the shifter go, her fingers tingling as the blood returned to them, and laced her fingers with Blair's. "I'm sorry. I don't share a lot of my personal life with my family." She closed her eyes and let out a breath.

"But they know you're gay, right?"

"Absolutely." She whipped her gaze to Blair. "But if I give them a bone, they run with it and never let go."

Blair let out a hearty laugh. "I've never been described in quite that way before."

"I didn't mean—" Her choice of words was poor. She wouldn't blame Blair if she wanted to leave right now.

"I know exactly what you meant." Blair squeezed her hand. "We're just friends, right?"

"Right." But were they really only friends? The jolt that shot through her told her they were more than that.

"So, stick with that thought and everything will be fine." Blair's easy-going attitude seemed to calm her, as usual.

"I'll give it a go." She released Blair's hand and pushed open the car door. "But you don't know my family. They're relentless when it comes to digging for details."

Blair got out of the car and followed her up the walkway to the front door. Rachel stopped before she reached for the knob. "Maybe I should just kiss you right here and now. My mom's probably watching through the window."

"I'm game if you are." Blair raised an eyebrow. "But maybe we should simply leave it at friends until after I meet them? Then you can decide what you want to tell them."

What *did* she want to tell them—what *did Blair* want her to tell them? She didn't know how Blair could be so calm about the situation. "If you insist." That was the better path to take. She turned the knob and pushed open the door to find her mother standing on the other side.

"I thought maybe you were having trouble with the door. It's been sticking lately." Her mom's lame attempt at covering her tracks was amusing.

"Seems to be working fine tonight." She twisted the doorknob back and forth before she closed it. "This is my friend, Blair...Uh... she's a friend of mine." *Way to repeat yourself, idiot.* Who was she trying to kid? She was much more than a friend now. Bringing her to Sunday dinner solidified that fact.

Her mother pulled Blair into a hug. "It's nice to meet you. Just call me Gwen."

Her brother appeared from the kitchen and held out his hand. "Yeah." He glanced at Rachel. "It's nice to know Rachel has a *friend*. She never brings anyone home."

She scowled at her brother. "I have plenty. I just don't want to scare them away by letting them meet you." Nothing like making it awkward.

Blair shook Ben's hand. "I'm glad to be the first to experience whatever that wonderful aroma is coming from the oven." She brushed off the awkwardness easily.

"Roast beef." Her mom headed into the kitchen.

Blair immediately followed her. "Can I do anything to help?"

"Nope. Just have a seat." Her mom pointed to the chairs at the counter. "Everything is ready except the potatoes." Her mom lifted the lid, and steam floated out. "They just need to be mashed, and that's Ben's job."

Blair sat at the counter as Rachel poured them each a glass of red wine. "Ben has been the official potato masher since he was a teenager." She handed Blair one of the glasses and sat next to her.

Blair was acting like she'd been here a thousand times before, which made Rachel like her even more.

Ben was full on into mashing when her father appeared from the garage. He didn't acknowledge any of them as he went to the refrigerator, grabbed a beer, spun off the top, and took a long pull. "What time's dinner?"

"In a few minutes." Her mother spun around. "Rachie's brought a friend tonight."

"I see that." Her father moved quickly across the kitchen and held out his hand. "Bob Taylor."

"Blair Haskell. Nice to meet you."

"Likewise." He glanced at Rachel. "You work with Rach?" Here came the third degree, one of the reasons Rachel didn't bring many people home to meet her family.

"Actually, no. I own a freelance bartending business."

"Been doing that long?" Her dad got right to the point, as usual.

"It's new, but I'm doing okay."

"Doesn't sound very stable. What's your ROI?"

"Dad." Rachel's voice rose. "Blair didn't come here to be grilled about her business profits."

Blair gave her a sideways glance. "It's okay. I've got some good competition, but the market is large, and I can handle it. All my equipment is paid for, and I've pulled about fifty percent of the jobs available in the last month." Blair didn't flinch at the questions. She was calm as she defended her livelihood to Bob.

"That's good. Give Rachel one of your cards, and I'll put in a good word for you at my firm." He proceeded to the table and took his usual seat at the head of the table. "Benny, you going to carve the beast?"

"On it." Ben retrieved the fork and carving knife from the block and began slicing the roast.

Rachel was glad to get the inquisition out of the way before dinner. Conversation was always awkward during the meal if it continued. Her dad seemed to be satisfied with Blair's answers and actually willing to help her, which meant she'd impressed him with her direct response. She'd kind of impressed Rachel with it as well.

Most people were caught off guard and stumbled to find the right words to answer.

"What are you working on in the garage?" Her father built furniture to wind down when he was home. His stress reliever helped him think through his work.

"Starting a table like this for your brother." He slid his hand over the smooth, glossy finish of the walnut table.

Blair popped up from her seat at the bar and sat at the end of the table next to him "You made this?" She slid her hand across the finish just as Rachel's dad had done. "This is magnificent. It must've taken forever."

Her dad beamed. "Sometimes it's hard to find just the right piece of wood, but once it gets delivered, it doesn't take long to make it happen."

"I thought I was getting the next table." Her dad had promised her one after he finished this one.

"That was the plan, but I was offered a larger piece of wood than I expected, and it was too beautiful to cut. It'll fit your brother and his family better. I have smaller piece coming next week that will work for you."

"Dinner's ready." Her mother motioned to the food on the stove. "Fill your plates and find a seat." She nudged Ben. "Get the kids in here, and I'll fix their plates."

"How do you know I won't need a bigger table?"

Her dad got up from his seat. "I never thought about it. I was thinking in the present. Are you planning to have kids soon?"

She could feel Blair's eyes on her but didn't dare look at her. She'd gotten herself into a conversation she hadn't planned to have tonight—especially in front of Blair. "Not soon, but you can make me a new table when that happens." *When...she'd said when. What the fuck was she talking about?*

The kids filed into the kitchen right on cue. She popped up from her seat and helped her mother fill their plates as they waited. They each got a plate of roast beef, mashed potatoes, and some kind of vegetable. Corn for the majority, but the youngest preferred green beans.

Once the kids were served and seated at the table, she took a plate from the stack and handed it to Blair. "We're not very formal here." There always seemed to be more people than expected.

"It's warm and comfortable. I love it." Blair touched Rachel's arm and then began filling her plate. "This looks delicious."

Rachel followed her through the line of food, and they seated themselves next to each other across from the kids, who filled an entire side of the table. She watched them eat. Ben junior, the oldest at twelve, was shoveling in his food so he could get seconds, and the twins, Jenny and Jack, age ten, were eating ridiculously slowly. They pushed their meat around their plates, avoiding it as they ate mashed potatoes. Delilah, the youngest, age seven, who seemed destined to be a vegetarian, was eating her huge pile of green beans before she touched anything else on her plate. Rachel had never ruled out children, but she'd never planned on them either. It was something to consider in the future—something to see if Blair was considering as well.

Blair had made it through the rest of dinner and the cleanup successfully unscathed. They'd just sat down in the living room when a petite brunette rushed through the front door.

"Lori. I thought you weren't coming tonight?" Rachel seemed alarmed and a bit confused. "I mean, Mom specifically told me that you had a candle party. Sorry. I forgot about it."

"That's fine. You can order something from the catalog." Lori fished a booklet out of her purse and held it up before she set her purse on the entryway table. "When Ben messaged me that you'd brought someone with you," she stared at Blair as she came into the room, "I finished up as soon as I could to get over here." She dropped the candle catalog onto the coffee table, then sat on the arm of the couch and gripped her thighs. "I'm Lori, Ben's wife."

"I'm Blair." She didn't elaborate on who she was in relation to Rachel. That was still undetermined. "It's nice to meet you."

Lori continued staring. "It's just so unusual for Rachel to bring someone home for dinner."

Blair smiled. "So I've heard." She'd heard a lot of new things about Rachel this evening.

"How did you two meet?" Lori seemed to be asking all the questions she'd missed earlier during dinner.

"We met at an art event." Rachel shook her head. "We've already been through this."

They'd agreed beforehand that a chance meeting in a gallery would beg less questions than telling her family they'd met during Rachel's trip to Las Vegas.

"I'm sorry. I missed the dinner conversation." Lori looked at Ben. "You'll have to fill me in later."

"There's nothing to fill in." Rachel picked up her glass and stood. "We're dating. Okay?" She went to the kitchen, came back with a freshly opened bottle of wine, as well as a glass for Lori, then topped off her mother's before holding it up to see if anyone else wanted any.

Blair covered her glass with her hand and let Rachel's statement sink in. This was new information. She wasn't opposed to it, but they hadn't talked about dating. They hadn't talked about next steps at all. Sex with Rachel was a spectacular experience, and she also enjoyed her company, looked forward to it even—sometimes more than sex.

"I've been trying to get that out of her all evening." Ben raised his hand to give Lori a high-five.

"That's great news," Lori said with a grin as she slapped her hand to Ben's. "How long have you been seeing each other?"

"A few months." Blair tilted her head and looked at Rachel. "Isn't that about right?" She counted the time from when they'd first met. It didn't sound so new that way. It really didn't feel new.

Rachel nodded as she returned to her spot on the couch next to her. "I think so."

She leaned closer and whispered in Rachel's ear, "I'm learning all kinds of new things tonight."

"Don't listen to anything you've heard." Rachel grinned. "It's all lies."

"I doubt that." She gave Rachel a twisted grin.

"Finish your wine, so I can take you home and do naughty things to your body." Rachel's low, sexy tone sent a tingle through her.

THE PROBABILITY OF LOVE

Blair gulped the last bit in her glass and stood. "I'm sorry to cut this evening short, but I have an early day tomorrow." A total lie, but she didn't have to be offered naughty things twice. She took her glass into the kitchen, washed it, and left it to dry on the drainboard.

Rachel was waiting for her at the door when she walked back into the living room. Seemed she was in a hurry to get into bed as well.

"Thank you so much for dinner and the company."

Gwen stood and gave Blair a hug. The rest of them did the same, except for Bob, who offered his hand again. It was like a receiving line at the weirdest wedding ever. Dinner with Rachel's family had been more pleasant than she'd imagined, even with all the questions.

On the way to the car, Blair laced her fingers with Rachel's. "It's okay. I'm good with dating as long as you are."

Rachel smiled and squeezed her hand. "Okay then. We're good."

Right now, in this moment, Blair couldn't disagree. Everything between them felt perfect.

CHAPTER TWENTY-THREE

Rachel had just arrived home from work and was about to order in dinner when she received a text from Blair.

Sorry. I got called to work a shift. Won't be able to make dinner tonight.

Disappointment hit her hard. Rachel had planned a nice dinner and movie for the night. Well, as nice as brick-oven pizza could be. They hadn't been able to spend the evening alone together in a few weeks, and that had been at her parents' house, so technically not alone. She'd been looking forward to it all day.

Tell them to call someone else.

They really need me. I've already said yes. I can't back out now.

I'll pay for your time, if that's what I have to do. She was tired of spending her evenings alone. *It's one night. No one will care.*

I care, and I can't believe you just said that.

What? It's a bar. Who's going to miss you if you can't come in?

I'm done discussing this. Don't wait up. I'm sleeping at my place tonight.

WTF? She waited to see if the bubbles appeared, but nothing did. *Fine. I'll find something else to do.* Rachel jammed her phone into her back pocket and took off out the door. After flopping into the driver's seat and slamming the door, she didn't start the car. She didn't know where to go or who to talk to. She couldn't keep discussing her sex life with Chloe. That was beginning to feel weird. Her mom was still out of the question. She always wanted everything to be perfect, and what she had with Blair was far from perfect right now.

She fired the engine and just drove, soon finding herself back at the hospital. The physical-therapy department there was open until eight o'clock during the week to accommodate patients who worked nine-to-five jobs.

Amy startled when Rachel walked through the physical-therapy-room door. "What are you doing here? I thought you planned to stay in tonight?" She seemed to be done with her patients for the night.

"I did, but Blair had to work." She didn't want to be at home *alone*, and work was really the only place she had to go. "And I have a few things to catch up on here."

"You sound upset." Amy found a squirt bottle of disinfectant and a towel and started wiping down the equipment. "Didn't you say you were keeping it casual?"

"I was, but we're kind of dating now, and this situation is exhausting. Late nights and early mornings don't agree." She paced the floor. "Plus, I like her too damn much. She's funny, smart, and ridiculously sexy."

"So, what's the problem?" Amy asked.

"I got upset that she was called in to work tonight at the last minute."

"So apparently casual is out the window now. You've been struggling with this situation for a while."

"I know. I took her to Sunday dinner at my parents' house." She shook her head. "We agreed to keep it casual—no dating, just sex—and to tell my family we're just friends, but then I told *everyone* that we're dating. I even think of her as my girlfriend now, which has changed all my expectations of our arrangement."

"Sounds like you derailed your own plan. She's spending the night at your place and vice versa, right?"

"All the time."

"Are you seeing other people?"

"No." She put her hand to her forehead. "When in the hell would I have time for that?"

"Seems like you have your evenings free. Is she seeing other people?"

"I don't think so, but I have no idea. I've never asked her." She paced as jealousy shot through her. "She could be, I suppose. She meets plenty of women at the bar. That's where we met in Las Vegas. Maybe she's not working at all."

"Hold on. Let's not spiral this into something crazy. It was just a question. She's probably not, so don't freak about it."

"I hope she's not seeing anyone else." Her stomach rumbled. What was happening to her? She'd never been jealous before. She'd had to get that emotion in check when she realized Shay was going back to Chloe. Why couldn't she do the same now?

"Then you need to start being honest with yourself. Your left brain needs to start listening to the right."

"I was a jerk tonight. Offered to pay for her time."

Amy's eyes widened. "How'd that go over?"

"It didn't. She got pissed. Stopped texting back."

"Can't say that I blame her. You just cheapened her livelihood and everything happening between you two." Amy stacked the newly delivered clean towels in the cabinet. "Are you *trying* to push her away?"

"No. Not at all. I honestly wanted her to come over—spend time with me tonight, just watch TV together. I don't have a filter sometimes."

"Sounds like you've entered into the wild nights of a relationship."

Had they—had she? "I don't know if Blair would agree."

"Maybe you should ask her?"

She ignored the question. "She works too much and throws every dollar she makes back into her business without saving anything for emergencies."

"Some people aren't fortunate to have a college education like we do."

"I wasn't even thinking about that." She hadn't been making comparisons but was clearly having issues differentiating between their two career choices. "I'm a complete ass, aren't I?"

"With a capital A."

"What do I do now?"

"Apologize?"

"After what I said, I don't even know how to approach that subject."

"Starting with 'I'm sorry' always works for me." The lilt in Amy's voice told her she was right but didn't want to push her.

"You make it sound so easy." She paced the room again. She needed something tangible to let Blair know she was serious. "I'm thinking about changing to ten-hour shifts." It took thirty minutes to get ready in the morning and twenty minutes in traffic each way. Changing to four ten-hour days would save her roughly an hour each week, and she'd have an additional day off to spend with Blair.

"I doubt that will solve your schedule issues or your exhaustion." Amy put the spray bottle on the table and tossed the towel into the hamper before she lifted herself onto one of the PT tables. "I have an idea. Why don't we switch shifts for a while?" Her legs swung beneath the table as she spoke. "Then you can sleep in and have more time with Blair in the mornings."

"Would you do that for me?" She'd always thought Amy liked the extended evening hours. She'd been doing it for ages and hadn't asked to change them, even after she'd had her first child or her second.

"Of course. Then I'd be home for dinner with the kids. We can always trade on days one of us needs to or switch back permanently if it doesn't work out."

"Okay. Thank you." Maybe that arrangement would solve some problems for them both.

"Great. You wanna start tomorrow?" She slid off the table. "Go find your girl tonight—apologize for being a jerk." She raised her eyebrows. "Maybe let her know how you're feeling."

"Yeah. I definitely need to do that." She didn't like the way the text conversation had gone earlier. Her anger hadn't justified her shitty response.

"I'm going to lock up." Amy pushed her toward the door. "Be honest with yourself and her."

"I'll try." She needed to be at least that if she had any chance of continuing this arrangement or anything else with Blair.

❖

Rachel hadn't expected how difficult it would be to get into The Speak Easy. Blair had told her there were specific entry requirements, but she hadn't paid that much attention to what they were. When she finally made it inside, she took a seat at a table away from the bar. She hadn't quite gained her courage yet and couldn't find an open space at the bar. Blair was crazy busy making cocktails. She watched in awe as Blair juggled drink orders. Now, she felt bad that she hadn't even been here to see where Blair worked. She'd never considered how hard Blair was trying to make ends meet.

A server appeared in her path of vision, and she kinked her neck to look around her. "You should stay a while. She puts on an awesome show."

"She certainly does."

"Used to be the bar's biggest draw, but she's started her own biz, and we can't get her to work many nights anymore unless it's an emergency."

"And tonight was an emergency?"

"Yeah. One of the regular bartenders is down with a stomach bug, and another was going to be late." The reasoning behind Blair's text earlier.

"Impressive." Behind the bar was Blair's safe zone. She was completely in control, perfectly calm throughout all the chaos. Rachel could never be like that in any situation.

"What can I get you to drink?"

"Corona, please." She watched Blair move down the bar from customer to customer and then to the server station, where multiple customers stood in the way.

"Lime and salt?"

"Yes." She nodded. "Oh, and I'm going to move up to the bar." She pointed to the end that Blair had worked, where a customer had just vacated a stool.

"Gonna give it try, huh?" The server chuckled.

"Is she single?" She couldn't keep from digging.

"If you'd have shown up a few weeks ago you might've had a shot, but I think she's seeing someone now. She's been pretty guarded about her time lately." She glanced at Blair. "I had to beg to get her to come in tonight."

That's all she needed to hear. Blair was hers, and people knew she was taken. Now to make up for being an ass earlier. It was clear that she was awesome at her job and the bartenders valued her more than Rachel did. Big mistake.

❖

Blair couldn't get Rachel's text out of her head. *It's a bar. Who's going to miss you?* The words resonated as she let the draft flow into the beer glass. She scanned the bar. Every one of these people would miss her, wouldn't they? And then the next text hit her. *I'll find something else to do.* Was that a threat? She didn't understand it—didn't know quite how to deal with it. She set the beer in front of the customer, took his payment for the three-dollar draft, made change for a twenty, and set it on the counter.

The bill waving in front of her brought her out of her thoughts. "I only gave you a ten."

Her mind was clearly not on work tonight. "Oh. Thanks." She slid the bill under the clip of the register. Her feet hurt, and all she'd wanted to do was curl up and relax with Rachel tonight. Now she didn't even know if she wanted to see her at all.

Someone tapped her on the shoulder as she finished rimming a beer glass with lime and salt. "I'm here, but can you hang out for a bit until we get through this rush?"

She popped the top off the Corona bottle and set it on the server tray. "Sure. I need a bathroom break, though." She headed into the back without waiting for an answer. She didn't have to pee but hadn't left the bar since she'd arrived several hours ago. The rush had been steady, and she didn't see it letting up anytime soon. She needed to clear her head—get Rachel's texts out of it. She couldn't blame her for being upset. She'd hoped to have a nice relaxing night at home as well, but what was she supposed to do? Just give up income? That was money in her pocket that she needed to pay her rent—to put food in her refrigerator. Her job wasn't steady like Rachel's. Not yet, anyway.

What hurt the most was that Rachel didn't value her work as much as she valued her own. Expected her to blow it off like she had paid vacation or sick leave. It *was* last-minute, but Rachel would never say no to someone who called needing therapy or default on any work commitment at the hospital in general. Blair didn't know if she could continue this arrangement if Rachel didn't support her in her goals.

She glanced at the clock on the wall. Time to get back out there. She loved her job but wasn't feeling much joy in it tonight. She pushed through the curtains to the front and glanced to one end of the bar and then the other. Her stomach jumped when she saw Rachel staring back at her. The usual reaction, but at this moment, she wished she could control it more.

She took in a breath to settle herself as she walked slowly toward her. Heat burned at the back of her neck as her anxiety flared. Was Rachel checking up on her—making sure she was really working? Would she be able to swallow her pride if Rachel wasn't ready to apologize for the things she'd said earlier?

"I didn't expect to see you here tonight."

Rachel smiled slightly. "I didn't expect to be here tonight. Thought I'd be at home snuggled up with you on the couch watching a movie."

More guilt. "I can't do this here." She turned, scanned the customers' drinks on the bar.

"Wait." Rachel clasped her arm. "I thought I could do this no-strings thing, but I can't. Something's changed—I've changed."

Blair's stomach clenched. She'd been thinking the same but hadn't figured out what she wanted yet.

"I want more than just sex." Rachel didn't lower her voice or even seem embarrassed when the couple sitting next to her began to stare. "I like the way things have been happening between us. Pizza—movie nights—just sleeping sometimes."

The knot in Blair's stomach loosened. "Me too."

"I've never committed to any relationship before, but I really want to do it with you, or at least try."

She lifted her hands. "This is my job. Can you handle it?"

Rachel's blank stare didn't give her much hope. "I changed my shift at the hospital. I'm going to start working twelve to eight."

"Really?" Blair was confused and a bit elated. Just a few minutes ago she'd thought they might have to call it quits.

"Really," Rachel said softly as she nodded. "I thought that would give us more time together, and I really want more time with you." She leaned across the bar, captured Blair's face in her hands, and kissed her. "I hope you do too. I mean, want more time with me."

Rachel held onto Blair's face, remained there for a moment, staring into her eyes as her warm breath flowed across her lips.

Blair kissed her again, happiness exploding inside her. That was the best news ever. Rachel had made a move to be with *her*—to make life easier for *her*. She hadn't prepared herself for this at all. In fact, just the opposite. Now she was sure of where this relationship was going, and she felt really good about it.

After Rachel released her, a random guy moved into the spot at the bar next to her. "Haven't I seen you somewhere before?" he asked, spoiling the moment.

Rachel glanced at him briefly. "Yes. That's why I don't go there anymore." She rolled her eyes and focused back on Blair. "I'm gonna go home now." She backed away from the bar and hooked her thumb over her shoulder.

Apparently, Rachel didn't mince words with douche bags, which made Blair happy. All she could do was grin. Her worries were gone, and life was good now. She ducked under the flapper of the bar and followed Rachel outside the bar and into the breezeway. "I thought this conversation would go so much differently."

"I know. I was an ass before, and I'm sorry." She kissed her gently. "Wake me when you get home, and I'll heat the pizza."

She watched Rachel get onto the elevator before she spun and went back to the bar.

"Wow. That was so sweet." The couple at the end of the bar were clearly interested in the outcome of the show.

"Yeah. It was." So far off from what she'd thought was next for them.

The woman smiled widely. "I feel like we should be invited to the wedding."

There wouldn't be a wedding anytime soon, but for the first time in her life Blair thought she might have a future with someone.

The other bartender approached her. "I can handle this. Why don't you go home? Have more than sex with your girlfriend?"

She planned on doing exactly that for the rest of the night and into the morning. She rushed into the back room, grabbed her keys, and sped out of the bar.

CHAPTER TWENTY-FOUR

Just over a week later, Blair had almost finished making a drink when she felt her phone buzz in her back pocket. She took it out and saw a text message from Rachel. *Can we stay at your place tonight?* Bubbles appeared on the screen. She wasn't done typing. *Chloe has a show opening in Kissimmee.*

She quickly typed. *Sure. Aren't you working late tonight?*

I traded shifts with Amy so I could go.

Why hadn't Rachel mentioned that fact to her before now?

I wish you'd told me. I would have arranged my schedule differently. Do you want me to see if I can get off early to go with you? Since Rachel had changed her schedule, Blair had been working through happy hour to earn extra income, and tonight she was filling in for someone else until nine. The booze was cheaper for the customers, so the tips were better.

No. You don't have to do that. I'm taking Shay.

That news hit her harder than she'd expected.

Another message came through quickly. *I thought I told you about it.*

She hadn't, and that bothered her. She rushed to the back room of the bar and hit the button on her phone for Rachel.

Rachel answered immediately. "Hi." She sounded as though everything was normal, but it wasn't.

"Why isn't Shay going with Chloe?"

"The usual. Chloe is going early to set up, and Shay doesn't want to show up alone."

"That's a little ridiculous."

"It's an arrangement we've had for a long time."

"I don't want you to go." Not without her.

"You're working, so what difference does it make?"

"I don't want you to take Shay...like she's your date or something."

"She's not my date. You know that. We do this all the time. Am I just supposed to sit home alone while you're at work?" Rachel was obviously just blowing off her feelings.

"Do you plan to break up their marriage or just wait around until it disintegrates on its own?" The comment was totally uncalled for, but Blair was angry.

"What are you talking about?"

"It's obvious that you're still in love with her. Whenever she calls, you jump—do whatever she wants."

"That's not true. This event was planned long before you and I began seeing each other. I can't cancel on her now."

"Even though I asked you not to go?"

"Don't do that. It's not fair." Rachel's voice was flat.

"Is it fair that it was planned long ago, and you didn't tell me about it or ask me to go with you?" She remembered the phone call she'd overheard in Las Vegas, when she'd thought Shay was Rachel's girlfriend. She was afraid Rachel would never get over Shay and be fully committed to their relationship.

"I honestly forgot about it until a few days ago, when Chloe reminded me. By that time, I knew you were already scheduled to work."

"I have to go." She had to hit the end button before she said something more that she'd regret. Blair was right back in the spot she was before. She didn't know if she could be with someone who disregarded her feelings so easily. Who would choose to go somewhere with someone else even after the woman she was sleeping with on a regular basis asked her not to?

Blair watched the clock at The Speak Easy, impatient to finish her shift tonight. She'd been stewing over her conversation with

Rachel. Why would she think it was okay for her to escort another woman's wife to an event—a woman she'd clearly had a thing for—even when she was technically single? Chloe had to have issues with that arrangement too. Blair had to make an appearance at the event somehow, but the bar was busy, and she couldn't leave yet.

A random dude scoped out the woman she was serving as he approached the bar. "Is this seat empty?"

The woman eyed him as she nodded. "This one will be too if you sit down." She'd mentioned to Blair earlier that she was waiting for someone.

"Nice comeback." She gave the woman a high-five as the guy turned and slithered off to his friends.

Another dude from the same group immediately replaced him. She couldn't wait to hear what the woman's comeback would be this time.

"I'll have a draft." He didn't even glance at her. Maybe there were still some nice guys around. She filled a glass with the draft on tap and slid it in front of him.

He leaned closer and whispered, "Can I get her name?" He tilted his head toward the woman as he dropped a ten-dollar bill onto the bar.

They never stop. "Why? Don't you already have one?" She took the guy's ten and slid it into the cash register, made change, and dropped it into the tip jar. No change for jerks.

"What's up with you tonight?" Hugo, the other bartender, bumped her shoulder. "You don't seem to be having as much fun with your zingers."

"I'm just not into it. Besides, the lady at the bar is doing great on her own."

"He's back." Hugo motioned to the first guy that had hit on the woman.

"Another beer?" Blair was nothing but pleasant.

The customer nodded, put his elbows on the bar, and leaned forward. "Did it hurt when you fell out of the sky?"

She rolled her eyes. If she had to listen to one more cheesy line from this guy, she was going to spill his beer on him.

Hugo walked behind her and mumbled, "Come on. Give it to this douche bag."

Not to disappoint, she went right back at the guy. "No, but it's going to hurt your ego when I kick your ass out of this bar."

"There's my girl." Hugo stepped in front of her.

The customer waved Hugo over. "She's flirting with me, right?" Obviously inebriated, he spoke louder than necessary. "I think she likes me."

"Listen, man. You can stop thinking. She doesn't *like* you, and even when she's nice to you that doesn't mean she wants to fuck you. This is her job." He shook his head. "Anybody who's ever fucked a bartender *did not* need to ask if the bartender was flirting. That's clearly not the case here, so if you and your friends can't be respectful, you need to take your party somewhere else."

The customer held up his hands. "Sorry. No disrespect intended." He glanced back at his laughing friends, then at Blair and the woman whose friend had joined her. "We were just having a little fun."

"Okay." Blair turned to Hugo. "Listen. I'm going to call Morgan to see if she can take over for me. I need to take care of something."

"Maybe she'll be better at the comebacks tonight." Hugo was always in to punish shitty customers.

"She probably will be." She took out her phone and sent a text to Morgan. *Can you cover for me at The Speak Easy for a few hours tonight?*

After a few minutes her phone buzzed in her pocket. *What time?*

Now to nine. It was a little after seven, which should give Morgan time to get there, and then she could make it to the event before it ended.

Okay. I'll be there in a bit.

Can I borrow a shirt? Her black pants would be fine, but the long-sleeved polo wouldn't fit the occasion.

Sure. Where are you going?

Art opening. Nothing too fancy.

Gotcha. See you soon.

Thanks!

She slid her phone back into her pocket. Morgan would bring her something appropriate to wear. She had a great sense of style.

❖

Rachel hadn't given Blair the address to the show, so she'd had to search the internet to find the location. Thankfully, Chloe had been creating a name for herself in the Florida art world and was listed in the event announcement. The show had come up early in her search. Once Blair had parked, she headed down the sidewalk to the gallery. She was almost to the door when Shay came through it and headed her way. *Fuck.* She didn't think the first person she'd see would be Shay. Rachel wasn't with her.

"Hey." Shay smiled when she recognized her. "I didn't expect you here tonight. Rachel said you had to work."

"I did, but I found someone to cover for me so I could make it by before the show ended." She glanced around her. "Where's Rachel?"

"Inside. I needed some air. Too many people in there for me." Shay sat on a bench in front of the gallery.

Blair sat down beside her. Maybe Shay could shed some light on this friendship. "Can I ask you something?"

"Sure." Shay smiled.

"You seem to have the best of both worlds—Chloe the talented wife, and Rachel the loyal best friend."

"I hadn't thought about it that way, but I guess I do." Shay scrunched her eyebrows together. "Does that bother you?"

As a matter of fact, it did. "Rachel has already told me that while you were in the hospital, through no fault of yours, she fell in love with you." She hadn't, but Blair had surmised as much.

Shay didn't respond, only stared at her. Maybe she wasn't aware.

"I'm going to be blunt. Does it upset you that she's fucking me when she's not catering to you?"

Shay blinked several times and shook her head. "She doesn't cater to me, and I don't expect her to. Contrary to what you believe, I want Rachel to be happy."

Was Shay really that shocked? "I would have to disagree with part of that statement. Rachel jumps every time you call." Didn't Shay know Rachel still had feelings for her, or was Blair totally off base to suspect that Shay enjoyed Rachel's attention?

Rachel came out of the gallery with two plastic glasses of wine and headed toward them. "When did you get here? I thought you were working late?" She handed one of the glasses to Shay and the other to Blair.

Shay looked up at Rachel. "She came to surprise you." She stood. "I better get back inside before Chloe misses me." Apparently, Shay didn't intend to mention the question she'd just hit her with. Maybe she did want Rachel to be happy.

"I told you that you didn't have to come."

"I wanted to." She took a sip of wine. She needed to know why Rachel didn't want her there. "I got Morgan to cover for me."

"Great." Rachel glanced at the door. "Let's go inside and look at the art." Rachel stood and moved toward the door.

So much for getting to the bottom of things.

Rachel stopped and reached out. "Come on. Chloe's got some really nice new pieces in this one."

That small gesture made everything better for a moment, but Blair still had questions—nagging questions that wouldn't go away until they were answered.

CHAPTER TWENTY-FIVE

Rachel was surprised yet happy that Blair had come to the show, but she could feel Blair watching her whenever Rachel glanced at Shay across the room. She just hoped it didn't get more awkward than it already was. She'd been keeping a close eye on Shay, because her anxiety kicked in regularly at these events—the whole reason Rachel continued to escort her to them. Soon enough she was going to have to stop being Shay's social crutch and leave that job to Chloe.

"I know Shay's your friend, but when you're somewhere with me, you need to be with me." Blair's tone was harsh.

"I *am* with you."

"No. You're not. You haven't been with me all night. You've been watching Shay."

"Well, I did come with her. I feel bad about leaving her alone. You can't fault me for that." She didn't want to upset Blair, but it was the truth.

"I just wonder if it would be any different if you'd come with me."

"You're not being fair." This whole evening just might blow up in her face.

"I think I'm being more than fair." Blair looked at Shay. "She's all yours." She spun and rushed out the door.

Shay immediately crossed the room and said, "She's upset that you came with me, isn't she?"

Rachel watched Blair race out of the gallery, torn as to whether she should follow her. "She is. I'm sorry."

"Don't be. It's not your fault. You should follow her." Shay pushed the curtain aside, went into the back room, and sank into one of the chairs. "I wish Chloe paid that much attention to me. Well, not the crazy-jealous part." She let out a soft laugh.

Rachel followed her into the back room. "I thought you two had resolved all those issues."

"We have for the most part. It's just that she's been working a lot lately, and I miss her."

"Why exactly are you talking to me about this instead of Chloe?"

"I'd like to know the answer to that myself." Chloe's voice became louder as she pushed through the curtain behind them. She must've seen Blair leave.

Shay gazed up at Chloe, and tears began to well in her eyes. "I don't know. I guess I didn't want to upset you."

"You not talking to me upsets me more." Chloe knelt beside her. "I don't want to end up where we were before."

All the relationship problems they'd had in the past stemmed from this exact situation—lack of communication.

"So, what do we do to stop it?" Shay wiped away the tears streaming down her cheeks.

"We go home and talk." Chloe stood and offered her hand to Shay. "Come on. They can do without me the rest of the night." She took Shay's hand before she glanced at Rachel. "You should go find Blair."

"Not sure she wants to see me right now." Or that she'd accept any kind of explanation. Even *she* didn't quite understand why she felt such an obligation to Shay.

"Go anyway. If you don't, you might lose her forever, and I don't think you want that. She's in love with you, and I'm pretty sure you're in love her too." Chloe raised her eyebrows and gave her a solemn smile. "You want us to drop you at her place?"

"Take my car." Shay stood and plucked her keys from her pocket and dropped them into Rachel's hand. "Chloe's right. Please go talk to her." She looked at Chloe and then back at her. "I don't want to cause your unhappiness."

"I will. I just need to figure out what to say."

"I've found that *I'm sorry* is always a good starter in situations like these."

"Yeah. I guess it is." It was becoming a phrase she used too often. Rachel watched Shay and Chloe weave through the crowd and out the door. Now she was all alone in a gallery full of people. She rushed to the door and found Shay's car down the street in the lot where they'd parked. She didn't want to be alone—she didn't want to be Shay's second any longer. *I'm sorry* was the least of what she needed to say to Blair.

Blair chided herself for letting this happen again. Why did she always seem to find herself in relationships with women who were still hung up on someone else? Last time she'd gotten off easy with Sophie and Tess. She hadn't committed her heart to anyone, but she'd totally screwed herself this time. All the signs were there. She just hadn't seen them—hadn't paid enough attention to even notice them—paid enough attention to her own feelings to realize she'd gotten in too deep. The fact that Rachel answered the phone whenever Shay called and she favored Shay's opinion over hers should have been the first clue. Hell, she even preferred to go to art events with Shay rather than her. Rachel had proved that point tonight.

When the doorbell rang, Blair couldn't imagine who would be at her door this late. She looked through the peephole, and her stomach clenched at the sight of Rachel standing—no, she was fidgeting on her porch. It was only ten o'clock. The event couldn't possibly be over by now. But there she was, looking as gorgeous as ever, and her heart did the usual flip-flop. She took in a deep breath to settle herself before opening the door.

"Why are you here?" And why didn't she just use her key?

"I didn't want to leave things between us the way they were when you left the gallery." Rachel brushed past her, didn't wait for an invitation inside.

"Yeah, well, with the state of mind I'm in, I'm not exactly sure where we are or where we're going to be in the future." She gave the door a shove, and it slammed shut. Not her intention.

Rachel spun around, eyes wide. "What state of mind is that?" She stared at her, waiting for an answer.

"Tonight was horrible for me. Watching you with Shay—not understanding why you're more aware of her needs than mine."

"I'm sorry." Rachel rubbed her forehead. "This is really hard for me."

"Being with me is hard for you?" Her stomach tightened. Even though she was thinking of ending this whatever-it-was herself, she hadn't planned for it to happen so quickly.

"You—me—all of it. I've been in the safe zone with Shay for so long I don't know how to get out of it. Can you understand that?"

"No. I can't." She shook her head. "All I see are huge red flags. My head and my heart are moving in totally different directions right now."

Rachel stepped closer and pressed her hand to Blair's chest. "I'm begging you to listen to your heart right now." She kissed her softly. "I think I'm in love with you."

She hadn't expected to hear those words. Not after Rachel's behavior tonight. "Really?"

Rachel nodded and let out a sigh. "Ever since I saw you again that night at the gallery, I thought there was something more between us. I just couldn't admit it then. And now after all the time we've spent together, I know there is for sure."

"I'm really scared, Rach. I can't go on being second best to Shay."

"You're not—never have been. I don't want to lose you."

"I don't want that to happen either." *I think I'm in love with you too. Just say it, stupid.* "I think I'm in love with you too."

Rachel smiled widely, then captured Blair's face in her hands and kissed her like it was the first time, only softer, sweeter, and full of love and tenderness. Blair's world tilted, and she tingled like someone had sprinkled a bag full of fairy dust onto them. She didn't want to ever lose this magical feeling.

Tears fell from Rachel's eyes as she broke the kiss. "No more escorting Shay to art events unless you're coming with me. I promise."

"What if she asks you to take her?" Would Rachel be able to resist?

"She'll have to go with Chloe from now on." Although Chloe had never mentioned any issues, she was sure Rachel's presence wasn't good for their marriage either. "Can we go to bed now?"

"Absolutely." She grasped Rachel's hand and tugged her to the bedroom. Just an hour ago she'd thought they were done, and now the evening crackled with possibility.

❖

Rachel moved closer as Blair unbuttoned her blouse and let it fall from her shoulders, then took Blair into her arms and kissed her. She trembled as she skimmed the curves of Blair's waist with her fingers. She let them travel farther up, let them circle around one breast, spiraling up to its peak before gently pinching the nipple with her fingertips. Blair gasped, and Rachel was instantly wet. She sucked Blair's other nipple into her mouth and was rewarded with a moan. She fell to her knees and trailed her lips down across the smooth, delicate skin of Blair's belly. Rachel's senses hummed as she felt the subtle, erratic tremors erupt from Blair. It felt wonderful to know she was making them happen. She returned to Blair's mouth and kissed her before Blair removed Rachel's shirt and ran her fingers down her arm, caressing her shoulder with her lips. Goose bumps rose on her skin, creating an orchestra of sensations for Blair to direct. Each touch sent an exquisite note singing through her.

Rachel kicked off her shoes as she unclasped her bra and let it fall to the ground before they continued to methodically undress each other—pants, then panties. Once Blair was undressed, Rachel stood back and looked at her, and let the usual tingle take over. "You're so beautiful." She didn't know what she would do without Blair to come home to—didn't want to live without her in her life. The steamy look Blair was giving her made her particularly vulnerable.

Blair tugged her closer. "Come here, gorgeous." Blair quivered as Rachel grazed her collarbone with her lips to the cut of her jaw and back again, then caressed her back with her fingertips. Blair's hands went to Rachel's hair as she tugged her in for another deep kiss.

They fell onto the bed, and Blair inched her way to the middle of it. Rachel crawled up next to her, heat radiating between them, and slipped her hand between Blair's legs. She felt the glorious, hot wetness as she dipped her finger inside. Blair thrust her hips against Rachel's hand. She added another finger and pressed her palm against her clit as she slid her fingers deeper. She gazed into Blair's emerald-green eyes as she eased her fingers in and out slowly. It wasn't long before Blair let out a deep, rolling moan as she threw her arm over Rachel's shoulder and bucked hard against her hand, holding her tightly as she rode out the orgasm. Watching Blair launch into orgasm was amazing.

Once the aftershocks subsided, Rachel gathered Blair into the crook of her shoulder and held her while she fell asleep. Satisfying Blair had become more gratifying than experiencing her own orgasm. She could spend every night slowly and methodically exploring Blair—touching, tasting, and experiencing her a thousand times more, as though she'd never done it before.

This lovemaking was sweet, soft, and gentle. It came from the heart rather than from a need for sexual gratification. Rachel couldn't suppress the sensations buzzing through her. This was much more than sex this time. This was the woman she longed for—the woman she loved. This was uncharted territory for her heart. She wasn't sure what the future held, but for now, they were heading in the right direction.

CHAPTER TWENTY-SIX

B lair's phone chimed several times, and she glanced at Rachel to see if the noise had woken her. Still out like a light. After their marathon of lovemaking, she didn't expect her to be awake. She slipped out of bed, put on her robe and slippers, then grabbed her phone from the nightstand and went into the kitchen.

The text messages were from Morgan. *You up? I'm coming by to drop off your tips.*

She typed in a message. *I am now. Bring food.*

Sweet or savory?

Both. Bagels with lots of cream cheese.

On it.

Don't knock. I'll unlock the door. She would let Rachel sleep a bit longer.

She shuffled across the kitchen to get the coffee from the pantry and then back to the coffeemaker. She filled the basket with coffee—this morning would be a full-pot day. She poured water in the top and pressed the on button before she went back to the bedroom and peeked inside. Rachel was still asleep—hadn't moved from the position she'd left her in. She breathed in a huge sigh of relief and pulled the door almost closed. Last night she'd thought it was all over between them, but it had turned out to be a new beginning—for them both. Rachel had opened up to her—released her vulnerabilities. Admitting her attachment to Shay hadn't been easy for Rachel, and distancing herself from Shay would be even harder.

The coffeemaker beeped as Blair returned to the kitchen. She retrieved several mugs from the cabinet and filled one to the brim. The scalding liquid burned inside her mouth as she sipped. She'd just lost all feeling in her tongue and probably all taste for an hour, but she didn't care. She needed caffeine—now. She took several plates from the cabinet, along with a large, shallow bowl, before she sat on the couch and sipped more of her coffee, staring out the window into the backyard. It was going to be a glorious morning—in fact, it already was.

She'd just clicked on the TV and muted it, to catch the weather for the day, when Morgan came through the door. She bolted from the couch and held her fingers to her lips, then waved Morgan into the kitchen. "Rachel is still asleep." She grasped one of the bags from Morgan's hand and emptied the bagels into the bowl she'd set out.

Morgan nodded as she unpacked the various containers of cream cheese and a small bottle of orange juice from the bag. "I got strawberry, maple-walnut, and plain."

"You got my favorite." She plucked a cinnamon-crunch bagel from the bowl, split it in half, and dropped it into the toaster. The aroma of burnt cinnamon and sugar filled the kitchen.

"And mine." Morgan retrieved an everything-bagel from a separate bag, then opened the regular cream cheese before she ripped off a chunk and dipped it into the container.

"I don't know how you eat those first thing in the morning." She pushed the cream cheese closer to Morgan. "You might as well take that with you. I'll never use it after you've contaminated it with all those flavors." She wasn't one for savory bagels in the morning. Lunch maybe, but never breakfast.

Her bagel popped from the toaster, and she pulled it out, her fingertips burning as she transferred it to a plate. Apparently cooking was dangerous this morning. She quickly slathered it with maple-walnut cream cheese and bit into it, moaning as the sweetness of the maple hit her mouth. She could eat these every day if her hips would let her.

"How'd it go last night after I left?"

"Good. Tips were better than I thought they'd be." Morgan reached into her pocket and pulled out a wad of bills, then laid the various denominations on the counter. "Hugo got on to that pack of dudes—made them pay up for the way they were acting." She gulped a swallow of juice. "Apparently they didn't mind." She moved the money around to reveal the twenty-dollar bills.

"Hugo's a gem, isn't he?" She picked up her coffee. "Thanks for coming in last night. I had some things to work out with Rachel."

"Sure. No problem." Morgan glanced at the bedroom. "She's still here, huh? I thought she'd be on her way to work by now."

"She changed her hours a while back so we can spend more time together."

Morgan grinned. "You look happy. She seems to have shaken up your plans a bit. Giving up extra work is going to cut into your business-plan timeline."

"My plans have definitely been stirred...but not shaken." She smeared the other half of her bagel with cream cheese. "I'm still planning to make my business successful." She just wished she didn't have to work so much to make ends meet.

"Even so, it looks like you're the one who made out from that bet." Morgan held up her juice and bumped it against Blair's coffee cup.

"I guess I did." She'd never really taken Morgan's bet, but she did win just the same.

Rachel appeared like a ghost from the next room. "Did I just hear you two say something about a bet—on me?"

"Oops." Morgan stilled.

Rachel came into the kitchen slowly. "Did you tell her everything that happened that weekend in Vegas?" She glanced at the money on the counter. "Just so you could win a bet?"

The back of Blair's neck tingled hot. "Absolutely not. I didn't tell her anything."

"Then what's all this?" Rachel stared at the cash.

Blair's stomach knotted as she glanced at the money—knew how it looked. "My tips from last night." She glanced at Morgan, hoping for some backup. "Tell her."

Morgan's skittish demeanor made her look guilty, which she was, but Blair hadn't been complicit. "It's what Blair said...her tip-out from last night." Morgan gathered her bagel and orange juice and sped to the door. "I'm gonna go."

"What the hell, Morgan?" She was totally making Blair look guilty.

"We can catch up later." Morgan was out the door.

Rachel stared at her silently for a moment. "I sure hope it was a good wager, because now you've lost it all." She rushed into the bedroom and started getting dressed.

The knot in Blair's stomach grew as she followed her. "Wait. It wasn't like that at all." She grabbed Rachel's arm. "Morgan bets on a lot of women when she's working."

"That's not an excuse for you wagering on me." Rachel fought with her shoes as she tried to get them on her feet.

"I didn't take the bet." She was pleading with Rachel. "I swear."

"I can't believe I opened myself up to you." Rachel rushed out of the bedroom, then stopped suddenly and turned around in the hallway. "Do you know how hard that was for me?" Tears welled in her eyes.

"I do, and I'm grateful. I would never do anything to hurt you." She tried to grasp Rachel's arms—make her pay attention.

"Well, that's not true—because you just did." Rachel swept the tears from her eyes.

"Rachel. Please listen to me." Her voice faltered, heated moisture searing her cheeks.

"I can't. I just can't." Rachel sped out the door and leapt into her car.

Blair slumped against the doorjamb for balance as she watched the love of her life screech out of her driveway. She rushed into the bedroom and threw on some clothes. It had taken her way too long to find Rachel. No way was she going to lose her over something that wasn't true.

Rachel's car wasn't in her driveway. She'd gone somewhere else, but where? Probably to Shay's house, and Blair wouldn't follow her there. That would only turn the situation into a huge explosion. She put the car in gear and drove to SoTess marketing.

There, she told Tess and Sophie everything that had happened just an hour before.

"Hmm." Tess fiddled with the pen on her desk.

"I let her set the pace—did everything right."

"Except you made a bet on her." Sophie's voice was low and accusatory.

"I didn't. I swear. I would never do that to any woman. That was all Morgan's idea."

Tess tilted her head. "I can see that. Why didn't you tell her no?"

"I did—several times."

Morgan stepped into the office with a tray of coffees. "She did. Always does." She set the tray on the table. "I should've kept my mouth shut."

"Yes. You should've." Blair paced the office. "I shouldn't have gotten involved with her. I warned myself, but she was a blaze of fire I couldn't resist."

"Don't say that." Tess stood and blocked Blair's path. "You can still fix this. She's bound to reason it out and realize you wouldn't do something that crude."

"She trusts you, doesn't she?" Sophie raised her eyebrows.

"I thought she did." Blair rubbed her head. "But we met in a bar. She could think I pick up women all the time."

"I doubt that."

"I would wonder." Sophie shrugged, and Tess glared at her. "I'm just being honest." She held out her hand. "Look at her. She's gorgeous. Probably gets hit on all the time."

"She does but doesn't take anyone up on it." Morgan handed Sophie a cup, then gave the other to Tess before she held the last one up to Blair.

Blair shook her head at the offer. She was so jittery at this moment that anything she put in her stomach would come right back up. "I just don't know why Rachel was so eager to believe the worst of me."

"Maybe she's been hurt before. Has she mentioned anyone in her past?" Tess held her coffee to her lips momentarily before she drank.

"No. Never. Except Shay, and she told me whatever feelings she had for her were gone." She'd thought they'd worked everything out last night. She hit the button on her phone to call Rachel again and held it to her ear. It went straight to voice mail. "I don't know what to do."

Tess rounded her desk, went to Blair, and rubbed her shoulders. "Do you want me to call her?"

Blair shook her head. "No. I appreciate the offer, but I don't think she'd like that."

"Okay. Then just give her a little time to think about things."

"Yeah." She agreed but worried that time would just make things worse if Rachel didn't believe her. Maybe this was Rachel's way out of the relationship. Maybe she wasn't convinced she should be in it in the first place. Maybe she really was still in love with Shay.

Rachel drove a few miles down the road and pulled to the curb on a random street in the subdivision. She shook as the sobs she'd been holding in engulfed her. She'd finally given her whole heart to Blair, and she'd broken it. Throughout their whole relationship—or whatever it was—Blair had deceived her. Blair had come to her room that first night in Las Vegas intending to win a bet, and even after they'd become closer, she hadn't told her anything about it.

Rachel searched through her purse for her phone, started to call Shay and Chloe, but she couldn't do that. How could she explain to them—to Shay—that she no longer found her attractive, and that the woman she'd been sleeping with saw her only as a perk from a bet? She shook her head. How could she be so stupid?

She scrubbed the tears from her face and hit the button for Amy. She'd been the voice of reason when she'd needed help recently. The phone rang a few times and then went to voice mail. She inhaled a deep breath and calmed her voice. "I'm coming by this morning, Amy. I need to talk." She hadn't even looked at the morning schedule and had no idea if she was busy.

She parked and headed into the hospital. She could only imagine her appearance. She hadn't even taken time to wash her face or brush her hair and was still wearing last night's clothes.

She veered her gaze away from the patient coming her way in the hallway as she headed to the physical-therapy department. Amy startled when she rushed through the door. "What are you doing here? I thought you were sleeping in with Blair these days."

"I just came from her place." She couldn't hold back the tears.

"Oh my gosh." Amy swept her into the office and closed the door. "What happened?"

"She made a bet with another bartender that she could get me into bed." She could barely get the words out between sobs.

"Are you serious? Do you really think she would bet on you?"

"Not now, but then...I don't know."

"So, what if she did?" Any shrugged. "Keeping it casual left the arena a while ago."

"Then how many other women did she bet on?" She rubbed her forehead as she paced the small office. "After we met in Vegas."

"I see your point."

"What if she's still betting on women? She's always out late—takes a shower as soon as she gets home." She was making up a whole scenario in her head.

"I guess she could be, but from what you've told me about her, I doubt it." Amy leaned against the desk. "She'd have to be superwoman to satisfy more than one woman and work the schedule she does. Remember how exhausted you were only a couple of weeks ago?"

"I just don't know what to do." Everything Amy said made sense, but she was still hurt by the whole situation and needed to know the truth. Her stomach rumbled.

"Take a few hours—or even a few days if you need to sort through it—but don't start making up reasons not to be with her. We both know you're in love with her."

She *was* in love with Blair. That's why it hurt so much. "I don't like being deceived."

"Maybe she was afraid to tell you, afraid this might happen. I mean, not long ago you offered to pay for her time, and she forgave you for that. Right?"

"Right." Blair had even left her shift early to come to the gallery last night. That was money out of her pocket.

"Seems to me you've been pretty happy since you met her."

"Right again." Maybe she'd overreacted. Amy had a way of making sense of it all. She paced the room again. She still needed to let this feeling of betrayal dissipate and had no idea how long that would take.

"Why don't you go home and talk to her? I'm sure you can work this out."

"I need to think about this whole relationship." Consider where it was and what she wanted from it.

"Okay. If you're not going home, then go get cleaned up and change into some scrubs. You can help me get ready for the new interns that will be starting next week."

"Shit. I forgot about them." They were plenty of help but needed lots of direction—a chore she didn't need right now.

CHAPTER TWENTY-SEVEN

Weddings usually made Blair happy, but her love life was coming out in every song played tonight, and it all seemed to be falling apart. She glanced around the room at the smiling faces. Even though she was surrounded by happy people at this small, family wedding, she still felt alone. Morgan wasn't available, had been MIA since blowing up Blair's relationship, so she was working the bar solo. She'd known Morgan's wagers would bite someone in the ass someday, but she'd always thought it would be Morgan. She was the player, not Blair.

The wedding was a small event she'd snagged at the last minute a few days ago. One person could handle this crowd, and that meant more money in her pocket. She'd bid the job months ago and hadn't heard back—had thought they'd gone with Cocktail City, her competition, but she'd contacted them again, and they were ready to contract with her.

During a lull at the bar, Blair took out her phone. No message from Rachel. Her fingers slowed as she typed the newest of many texts to Rachel. *Please talk to me.* She hoped it didn't go unanswered like the dozens of previous ones she'd sent during the day. Several times she'd seen bubbles appear, but not a single text had come through from Rachel.

She'd also left several voice messages explaining the money that Morgan had brought by and why they had even talked about a bet. What was the big deal, anyway? She hadn't taken it. They were together now, and they were happy, right? She thought they'd worked everything out the night before. They'd made love with a new, different kind of passion. It wasn't just sex. It was intimacy at a much deeper level. She wanted that forever, and she wanted it with Rachel.

She finished fixing several drinks for a few people, and they left the bar. She was cleaning the bar space when she looked up to see Paige, the owner of Cocktail City, hurrying around the circumference of the room toward her.

Paige narrowed her eyes as she neared. "You again."

Now she knew Paige had bid the job. "Having trouble attracting business?" It was a shitty thing to say, but she wasn't in the mood to play nice tonight.

"My business was great until you showed up and started undercutting me." Paige scanned the bar setup.

"Just trying to claim my piece of the pie." She wasn't doing it purposely. Blair had set her prices when she'd started the business and didn't plan to raise them to match the costs Paige had set for Cocktail City. She wasn't running a gas station with a competitor across the street.

"Well, now you're cutting into mine." Paige planted her elbows on the bar.

The music stopped, and suddenly the bar was slammed. Paige came around back and started helping with the drink orders. Blair hadn't expected that, and they actually worked well together. Paige handled beer and wine orders as Blair made a few mixed drinks. The crowd dispersed for the toast, and Paige just stood there and stared at her.

"I have to admit you're good." Paige seemed to be sincere. She'd gone from spewing accusations to giving compliments.

"Not my first rodeo." She didn't know what else to say, but maybe she should be more gracious. "Thanks."

"You and I need to talk. Meet me tomorrow at Coffee Central, nine a.m. sharp."

Blair raised an eyebrow. She wasn't keen on taking orders from her competition.

Paige blew out a breath as she closed her eyes momentarily. "Please? I have an idea to discuss that could help us both."

"I don't know if I can make it tomorrow. I'm dealing with a personal issue."

"Don't tell me. Your partner hates your work hours, right?"

"Something like that." She wasn't about to confide in someone she barely knew.

Paige glanced at Blair's phone behind the bar. "You've checked your phone a dozen times in the last thirty minutes. I saw you—I've been there myself. What I want to discuss might help that situation." Paige took a card from her back pocket and handed it to her. "Call me when you can meet."

"Okay." If Paige had any notion of taking over her business and becoming her boss, she wouldn't even consider it. She picked up her phone and slipped it into her back pocket. If Paige noticed her paying too much attention to her phone, then someone else would have as well. That wasn't good for business.

"I'm serious. Call me." Paige rushed around the perimeter the same way she'd come in.

A few minutes later Blair's phone buzzed in her back pocket. She whipped it out to see a text message from Rachel on the screen.

Stop texting and calling. I need some time to figure things out.

She had begun texting back when another text came through.

STOP.

The knot in her stomach tightened, and she shoved her phone into her pocket. If Rachel needed time, she would give her that. For now.

Blair approached Coffee Central, glanced through the window cautiously, and glimpsed Paige sitting at a table toward the back of the shop. She stopped and leaned against the building. She'd made it this far but still wasn't sure working with Paige was the right move for her business at this time. She still had some money in the bank, but it sure would be nice to have someone help with the finances. Yet if Cocktail City was struggling as well, Paige might not be any better at finances than she was. She pushed off the wall and headed inside. She'd listen to what Paige had to say but didn't have to agree to anything right now. What did she have to lose?

When Paige saw her, she immediately stood. "I'm glad you decided to meet with me."

"I'm not sure exactly what you want to talk about, but I'm willing to listen."

"Do you want something to drink…eat?"

"Just coffee." Blair had been pretty much living off caffeine these days.

Paige waved at the waitress. "Can we get another cup of coffee?" She motioned to her cup as she spoke.

The waitress appeared with one and a bowl filled with creamer containers.

"So, what's this idea you want to discuss with me?" She took a sip of her coffee and held in a hiss as the hot liquid burned her tongue.

"It seems we're both working the same areas, and I thought maybe we could reach some kind of an agreement."

"What kind of agreement?" Surely Paige wasn't going to ask her to line out a territory.

"I've been running Cocktail City for a long time, and it seems my methods are getting stale—must be, or I wouldn't be losing business to you."

"And?" She raised an eyebrow.

"And I'd like to propose a partnership." Paige sipped her coffee.

Blair hadn't expected that offer. "What would it entail?"

"We merge. Equipment, staff, finances—everything."

"I don't have a lot of equipment, and it's just me and Morgan working the events."

"I'm aware of that." Paige relaxed into her chair and crossed her arms.

"Why me? Plenty of other independents that you could ask are working the area."

"I've been looking for someone whose skill set complements mine, and you seem to fit that bill."

"How so?"

"First off, you're educated and certified." Paige uncrossed her arms and leaned forward. "You know how to ensure your guests have a great time without having too great of one. You know how to graciously ask for ID and how to help certain guests choose water over the next adult beverage."

"You've certainly done your research."

"I won't lie. I went to every event you underbid me on. I've been watching you for weeks."

"It *was* you." She let out a quick breath. "I thought it was just my imagination."

"I needed to see my competition. No one else has hurt my business as much as you have, and that puzzles me. I have a dozen bartenders more than you, and you're still booking a considerable number of customers I'd usually handle."

"I wasn't trying to hurt your business." Blair picked up her cup and then set it down again. "I'm only trying to make mine successful."

"You can't really make yours a success without pulling customers from me. There's only so much business in the area. Frankly, you're cutting into my profits more than any other business has in the past." Paige didn't seem at all hesitant. "Listen. I love what I do, and there's nothing I love more than helping people enjoy a good party. I've seen you in action, and you and I appear to be a lot alike in that way."

She couldn't attest to that comment since she hadn't been stalking Paige for the past few weeks.

"You and I both like to make people happy, right?" Paige's smile widened.

"I can't disagree with you. That's the best part of the job." She did enjoy making people happy—the reason she booked so many weddings. Everyone was in a good mood, and she didn't have to keep track of any tabs. It was even better when they hired a good wedding band or DJ. Sure, occasionally a wedding would go off the rails and the party would contain some combustible action, but most of them were drama free.

"Okay. Good. You can add value to my business, and, more importantly for you, I can add value to yours. We can work independently and struggle to make ends meet, or we can work together and be unstoppable." Paige held out her hand. "What do you say?"

Blair wasn't ready to commit to anything. There were too many unknowns. "What if we get three months down the line and it's not working out?"

Paige relaxed into her chair and crossed her arms again. "We'll need six months to see if we can be profitable. We can write a clause into the contract that states if either of us doesn't feel this is a good idea, at that point we can split with our own equipment and whatever percentage of money we brought into the deal." She leaned forward, picked up her empty coffee cup, and rolled it between her hands. "We'll still both have to hustle to bid the right events. Customers seem to really like you, so your part in getting jobs will be crucial. Having access to more staff should eliminate your crazy working hours and give you more time off to spend with whomever you were texting last night."

"It would be nice to have a more regular schedule." Not that she knew where anything stood with Rachel. They still weren't in contact—everything was up in the air.

"You'll probably be able to give up your side job at The Speak Easy as well."

"Jesus, you really have been stalking me."

"Actually, that information came to me. One of my staff interviewed there and happened to mention she saw you working the bar."

"I fill in when they need help." More than necessary lately. It would be nice to rely on only one job for income. Juggling two had been stressful.

"What do you say?"

"Sounds like you have everything worked out, so let's give it a try." Unless Blair was missing something, it sounded like a good deal.

"Great. I'd like to keep this as simple as possible so we can move quickly."

"I don't know if I can do that." This was a big change, and she'd really like to discuss it with Rachel.

"Come on. You're bleeding money. You have to be with the prices you're setting." Paige frowned. "I know it's not easy, but you have to step back and take a cold, hard look at where your business stands in the local marketplace—where it'll be a few months down the line." She scrunched her eyebrows together. "This is our chance to change that situation. It'll be epic."

Paige was right. Blair was struggling financially and really didn't have any other choice than to partner with her or call it quits. "Okay."

"Great. I'll get a contract together, and we can sign this week." Paige smiled lightly, seeming to sense her reluctance. "Trust me. I've been pondering this for a while, and I've done a lot of research. You and I can help each other achieve the highest level of success possible, and I don't say that to just anyone." Paige stood and held out her hand.

She took in a deep breath. "I hope this arrangement does what you think it will."

"It should exceed my expectations. It's a win-win situation."

Still unsure about the arrangement, Blair stood, took Paige's hand, and shook it. She didn't have many options.

CHAPTER TWENTY-EIGHT

Rachel scrolled through the notes in the records of each of the new interns. Even with some of the issues noted in several of their files, she was ready for them. They'd been super busy lately in the physical-therapy department, and the interns provided extra coverage when the clinic was overloaded. Interns always came with more risk, and she wasn't looking forward to bird-dogging them every day. The responsibility was huge. She literally had their future in her hands since they relied on her and Amy, as well as other staff, to teach them. If the interns didn't do what they were supposed to correctly, they had to write them up. Most interns performed well. Some were exceptional, and unfortunately some couldn't handle the pace and barely scraped by.

It wouldn't be the first time she'd had an intern who couldn't perform an assessment or treatment in a safe manner. She'd had many who couldn't sustain a caseload. Also a few had demonstrated a lack of critical-thinking skills, which had made her wonder how they'd gotten as far as they had. Mostly she found that interns had absolutely no social skills when it came to interacting with patients, their families, or other health-care providers. They tended to spend so much time focused on learning the sciences that they forget the importance of being personable.

Amy poked her head into the office and then came inside, closing the glass door behind her. "They're here." She sang the announcement in her happiest of voices.

"How do they look?" She glanced up from the computer screen at Amy, who sat on the corner of her desk with her arms crossed, scrutinizing the four newcomers—two women and two men.

"A couple are prima donnas." She pointed to each of them as she spoke. "One overachiever and one who looks like he just rolled out of bed."

She got up, walked around the desk, and leaned against it. "Your assessment seems to be spot-on."

"I haven't seen enough of sleepyhead to know whether he's been up all night studying or other things not related to learning."

"Well, why don't we take a look at his last rotation review?" She went back to her seat and pulled up the report. "Studying." She clicked into another review she'd looked at earlier and turned the monitor so Amy could see it. "Which one is she?"

"Prima donna with the light-brown hair." She blew out a breath as she studied the review. "She's going to be a challenge." She'd been counseled for letting others do work for her.

"Remember, the transition from student to working professional can be challenging at times. We have to provide people like these the opportunity to grow."

"Why can't they come to us already seasoned?"

"Then they wouldn't be interns, would they?" She punched a couple of keys on the keyboard to lock the computer. "Let's get to it." She pulled the door open and waltzed into the clinic with Amy right behind her.

"Good morning." Three of the interns gave Rachel their immediate attention, but one of them had to nudge the sleepyhead, who seemed to be asleep while standing.

"Good morning," they all replied in unison.

"I'm Doctor Rachel Taylor, and this is Doctor Amy Baker. Welcome to Largo Medical Center's Physical Therapy Department." It was time for the hard-ass drill. She always started that way to avoid any misunderstandings. "I expect you to arrive at least fifteen minutes before your shift to review your schedule and see if there are any changes. Remember, you have to be flexible and open to cancellations and reschedules." She glanced around the room to make sure everyone was listening. "You can count on seeing anywhere between fifteen and thirty-five patients during each eight-hour shift. Remember to wear comfortable shoes. You'll be on your feet *a lot*."

Amy continued the instructions. "If you notice any new patients on your schedule, review their initial evaluations, including what they're here for, their medical history, and their mobility goals. As an intern, you're part of this team, so we expect constant communication with patient service coordinators. They are your go-to people if you have questions regarding the day's schedule or your patients' insurance, authorizations, or medical records. Also, document, document, and document more. Patient records are an invaluable resource for other therapists and health-care professionals."

She handed each of them a tablet to view their patient charts. Every patient session focused on different treatments. On the first day alone, some of them would be exposed to many treatments they hadn't seen before. Today would be busy for all of them.

Time passed quickly as Rachel watched the interns work with the patients. They all seemed to be doing well, even the one with issues. The quality of treatment she was seeing from them was also astounding, but this was only day one. The sessions seemed comfortable and relaxed while still being productive.

One of the new regulars came through the door. Wheelchair-bound due to an accident, he had a broken hip and was doing well in therapy so far. She watched as blond prima donna raced across the room to mark her territory, smiling widely as she introduced herself.

"What's going on? You look like you're ready to pounce." Amy apparently didn't see what was going on.

Rachel glared across the room at Blondie as she helped the new arrival climb out of the wheelchair and steady himself between the parallel bars. "I can already tell that one's going to get too familiar with her patient."

"She's just being friendly. It's good that she has social skills." Amy watched Blondie across the room. "Wouldn't you agree that making a session feel like you're catching up with an old friend makes the patient more comfortable and the session more enjoyable for both?"

"Yes." She gave Amy a sideways glance. "Why do I feel like you haven't finished this lecture?"

"Because I haven't." Amy turned to her and raised her eyebrows. "Social skills and patient-relationship development are probably some of the most valuable skills in this field." She raised an eyebrow. "And might I remind you that you fell in love with a patient?"

"No one should do what I did. We both know how that worked out." She was hypersensitive to those situations now.

"But then you eventually let that attachment go and fell in love with someone else."

"You know how that's going too."

"Are you seriously still mad at Blair? Have you even talked to her?"

She shook her head. "No. I'm not ready. I still get sick to my stomach when I think about it."

"You need to forgive her and move on."

"It's not that simple. I need to sort out my feelings before I make my next move." She should probably be flattered, but she wasn't—she felt used.

"Your next move?"

"Before I decide what I want out of this relationship."

Amy shook her head as she tilted it. "I wouldn't wait too long, Rach. She's an attractive, successful woman. Someone might snatch her up while you're still stewing about a silly little bet."

"If she's that quick to let go, then I know exactly what I meant to her, don't I?"

"Why are you being such a hard-ass about this? If it was me, you'd be telling me to suck it up and move on with my life or get out of the relationship."

"I know." Rachel wasn't worried about the small stuff—whose turn it was to do laundry or make dinner. This was about secrets and trust. "If you've got this, I'm going to write some notes about my observations." She was done with this conversation

Rachel considered four factors when assessing intern performance. Concerns about safety and professional behavior, a student's clinical reasoning skills, and a lack of progression were key factors in recommending a final grade. She was more likely to recommend a failing grade if she noticed a series of repeated incidents rather than an isolated one. All in all, it had been a good first day—no major mishaps or issues. As of today, no one would fail except herself, for her inability to cope with her own personal issues.

CHAPTER TWENTY-NINE

Blair pulled into the industrial park and drove slowly as she viewed the address numbers, looking for the one for Cocktail City. Not too far from Tess and Sophie's marketing business, she finally found it at the very end of the building, parked, and went inside. No one was at the front desk, so she wandered through the open door into the warehouse. The area was larger than Blair expected. Her bar and inventory was like an Easy Bake Oven compared to the amount of equipment Paige had added to her business. Why was Paige interested in her small business? Maybe this was her MO—buy out the competition to corner the market. Was Blair just a small cog in the wheel of Cocktail City's expansion?

"Hey. I was glad to hear from you so soon—good to see you." Paige pulled her into a hug. A complete one-eighty from their interactions in the past.

"Hi." She backed up awkwardly and glanced around the room. "I had no idea you had this much equipment."

"Yeah. I purchased it all last year because business was good, and I had planned to expand." Paige crossed her arms and turned to face her. "And then you showed up in town."

"Just trying to make a living."

"Well, as I told you before, you took a good portion of my living." Paige blew out a breath. "Undercutting me by ten percent was a smart business move."

"Whether you believe me or not, my prices were independent of yours." It was clear now that Blair had set her prices too low.

Paige walked across the warehouse to a bar trailer that looked to be brand-new and ran her hand across the blank area below the window. "Do you know what this said before?" She glanced up at her. "Shake It."

"I *heard* they went out of business. Didn't know why."

"I tracked them and lowered my bids to steal anything they tried to book." She smiled confidently. "Then I bought all their equipment when it went to auction."

Wow. Paige was cutthroat. "But you didn't do that to me." She scrunched her eyebrows together. "Why?"

"Normally I would've, but I've seen you work the bar, and I'm impressed with how far you've come in such a short time."

"Do you usually spy on your competition?" Blair was still surprised at that tactic.

"Absolutely. It's the only way to keep up. I've also read your reviews. People seem to really like you."

Blair grinned. "That's good to know."

"I wouldn't have contacted you otherwise." Paige walked toward the office. "Come on. I'll show you my plan."

"You're pretty sure of yourself."

"Have to be or I'd never survive in this business." Paige went into the office and sat behind the desk. "If I gave up every time things got tough, I'd be working on someone else's budget in an office somewhere."

Paige was right about that. Several times recently she'd thought about quitting. "You have accounting experience?" Blair had taken a few classes but wasn't as budget savvy as she'd like to be.

"I have a bachelor's degree in finance."

So that's why Paige had been able to stay in business for so long—and to withstand the competition. "That's not my strong suit. The numbers get to me sometimes, and I have to walk away until my mind frees up enough space to work on them." If Blair was better at it, she wouldn't be here now.

Paige pushed a contract across the table at her. "With the number of customers you've stolen, I would've never guessed that." Seems she was a little bitter after all. "Maybe I should revise this?" She spun it around on the table and glanced at it briefly, then flipped it back to her. "This should do. The fact is, I want to work with you."

The first word she saw was partner. She couldn't possibly have enough capital in her business to justify being a partner. "You want to do this fifty-fifty?"

"I thought a lot about it before I approached you." Paige relaxed into her chair. "As I said, I *want* to work with you. I like what you can bring to the table. Your marketing skills are impressive." She didn't veer her gaze. "You moved here from Las Vegas, and within weeks of opening your name was everywhere."

Paige *had* done some research on her, but not enough, or she would've known that Tess had helped her with that. She'd take the credit for now. No sense letting Paige know that she wasn't as impressive as she thought. Tess had been very generous with her time and expertise when she'd encountered that hurdle. Getting your name out there was a huge feat, and Tess had created a campaign that had her phone ringing constantly.

She glanced at the contract, and her neck tingled at the legality of it all. She took a deep breath to settle her nerves. "I like what you're offering, but I need to look over this more thoroughly." It seemed good, but she didn't want to sign anything too fast. "Can I take this with me? Mull it over for a day?"

"I'd wonder about you if you didn't. It's a big step...for both of us." Paige stood, moved to the office door, and opened it. "Take a couple of days. Let me know when you're ready to sign. You have my number."

She stood. "Thanks."

Paige opened the door. "You know your way out?"

She nodded. Paige didn't seem to have any trust issues when it came to her inventory or her secrets. This might just be the best deal she'd ever been offered.

She got into her van, fired the engine, and immediately hit the call button on her phone for Rachel. It rang several times and then went to voice mail. "Rach, will you please call me. It's important."

She needed advice right now, so she drove straight to SoTess Marketing. Her knuckles whitened as she gripped the steering wheel. This was a huge decision, and she really wanted to talk it over with

Rachel. Or maybe that wouldn't be an issue—maybe they *weren't* together any longer. Surely Rachel wouldn't—couldn't just go on with her life without her—could she?

Blair could see though the window that Sophie was alone in the office when she arrived. She glanced at her watch. Tess had probably gone out to pick up something for lunch. She had no idea where Morgan could be.

Sophie glanced up when she came through the door. "Hey." She immediately stood, crossed the room, and pulled her into a hug. "How are you doing?"

"I've been better."

"Still no communication from Rachel?" Sophie raised her eyebrows.

Blair shook her head. "Nope. She won't return my calls."

"She needs to get over that shit." Sophie was always direct, didn't hide her feelings about anything, which was refreshing to some and annoying to others.

"I'm not sure what else I can to do at this point."

"So, what brings you here?"

"I need your help with something." She retrieved the contract from her bag and handed it to Sophie.

"You're going to sell your business?" Sophie rounded her desk and sat.

"Not exactly. I'm going to merge with someone else's."

"Oh. I didn't know you were considering a partnership." Sophie glanced up from the contract. "Did you tell Tess about this?"

She shook her head. "No. It just happened over the past couple of days. Paige, the owner of Cocktail City, approached me the other night, said she wanted to meet."

"I wonder what prompted that." Sophie flipped the page.

"I've been taking her customers."

Sophie grinned. "Good girl."

"Yeah. She's been losing money, and I really haven't been making enough." Clearly she hadn't been taking enough of Paige's business.

"Oh." Sophie glanced up from the contract. "I didn't realize that."

"There's just one of me, and I have Morgan only when she has time to work the events. I don't have enough revenue to hire anyone else except contract labor for large events." She let out a breath. "It's completely exhausting."

"The contract looks good to me." Sophie handed it back.

Tess came through the door holding a brown paper bag. "Hey. I didn't know you were coming by today." She set the bag on the table and fished out a few containers of sushi. "If you're hungry, we brought plenty for lunch." She glanced at Sophie. "Can you grab some drinks from the fridge?"

Sophie popped up and went to the small kitchen area adjoining their office. "Water or soda?" Sophie's voice floated through the space.

"Water." She and Tess responded in unison.

Morgan entered the office with another bag. "Hey. How's it going?" She took a large container of soup from the bag.

"Good." *Traitor.*

"Listen. I'm sorry for rushing out the other day. I just thought it would be better if you and Rachel talked it out alone."

"That didn't happen. We're currently not speaking." Blair couldn't hide her irritation.

Tess set all the containers in the middle of the table, then opened the one with the spring rolls, plucked one out of the container, and took a bite. "Can you grab some paper plates and a few mugs for the miso soup while you're in there?" She dropped a set of chopsticks and a fork, along with a napkin, in front of each of their spots at the table. "Go ahead. Eat something."

"Okay. Thanks." She plucked a piece from a container with the chopsticks and put it into her mouth. She wasn't really hungry until she saw the food. She hadn't eaten much in the past few days and probably needed to get something into her stomach. "This looks really good."

Morgan crossed the office to help Sophie with the mugs, then poured some soup into each one.

"Yeah. It's our favorite little place." Sophie brought the waters to the table and dealt the plates out like they were playing cards flying across the table. "And it's in walking distance, which makes it dangerous."

Tess laughed. "We spend way too much money there."

Blair chewed and swallowed. "Totally worth it."

"So, what brings you to our neck of the woods this morning?" Tess was always curious but didn't always ask what was going on right away.

"I'm planning to merge Blissful Bubbles with Cocktail City."

"Your competition?" Morgan raised her eyebrows. "Why?"

Blair plucked another sushi roll from the container. "We're both struggling, and we've agreed we'd do better together."

"Oh." Tess chose several pieces of sushi from the boxes and added them to her plate. "Have you made it legal yet?"

Blair shook her head as she chewed, then took a drink of water. "I brought the contract. Sophie checked it for me."

Tess glanced at Sophie. "Does it look good?"

"Yep. None of the capital will change ownership until their return on investment is up. So, if it doesn't work, neither one is out anything except their new business name." Sophie pushed a piece of sushi around on her plate. "Blair can go back to using Blissful Bubbles if she needs to."

"That's great." Tess glanced back at Blair. "Why do you look so sad?"

"I'm not sad. It's just a lot of change all at once. I need to move out of my place—find a more affordable house to rent if I'm going to make this work."

Tess raised her eyebrows. "You can stay with us until you find somewhere else."

"Oh, no. I couldn't do that. I'll find something. A cheap hotel, if nothing else."

"You absolutely will not." Tess glanced at Sophie. "We have an extra room, and you *will* use it."

"Okay." She'd forgotten what it was like to have friends she could count on. "It's kind of a short timeline."

"We'll make a plan to start moving you out this week." Sophie picked up her mug and sipped her soup.

It was amazing how together Tess and Sophie were in everything they did. She'd known how well they fit together socially, but they were also dynamic together in business. They were a damn powerhouse.

CHAPTER THIRTY

Rachel's anxiety was through the roof tonight, so high she couldn't even enjoy the art. She stood across the gallery staring at a painting of who-knows-what waiting for Shay to bring her a glass of wine. She'd finally told Shay about the situation with Blair, and Shay had reluctantly agreed to help her stay away from the bar and Blair tonight. They'd had no eye contact at all. Blair seemed to be avoiding her as well, but every time she looked her way, her stomach vaulted to her throat. Blair was probably having the same issue. It had been a hell of a first week with the interns, and Rachel wasn't up for more conflict with Blair.

Shay held the glass of chardonnay in front of her. "Why don't you just go talk to her?"

"I can't. I don't even know why I came tonight." She took the glass and sipped the wine.

"You knew she'd be here. You came because you wanted to see her." Shay turned and stared at the bar.

"Not completely true. I didn't want to leave you alone tonight." She'd struggled with the dilemma all day but finally decided not to hide from Blair any longer.

"That's bullshit and you know it." Shay rolled her eyes. "Don't use me as your crutch. I've been to plenty of these on my own, and I'm okay with being here."

"Are you saying you don't need me?"

"I'm saying that I'm not standing in the way of your happiness. *You are*, and I'm not sure why." Shay scrunched her eyebrows. "Are you afraid of committing to her?"

She shook her head. "No. I don't think so."

"Then what is it?"

"I don't know. It's just been a crazy week for me. New interns and all." She really *didn't* know. Everything she had with Blair had been wonderful. Why couldn't she get past this one little thing? Why couldn't she believe her?

"I'm not buying that. Not long ago you wouldn't have let work or anything else stand in the way of seeing her. You rearranged your whole schedule to have more time with her."

That was totally true. Life had been really good only a week ago. "Maybe I'm afraid of getting hurt." *Again.*

"Listen. You know how much shit I put Chloe through. It's a miracle she took me back at all—and still loves me. Bad communication hurt us both *a lot.*" Shay looked into her eyes. "You can't let a stupid bet stop you. Chances are you're going to hurt each other at some point, but I know from experience that if you love each other enough, you can work through it."

"Maybe so." She wandered to the next painting.

Another hour passed, and she and Shay had made it around the gallery twice, successfully avoiding looking toward the bar. She knew she was being childish, but she wasn't ready to talk to Blair. Not here.

"Hey there." Sophie appeared between them as they stared at the painting on the wall. "You two have been MIA for a while."

Rachel glanced at Shay. "We've been checking out all the new artists' works."

Shay shook her head. "That's an absolute lie. We've been avoiding Blair."

"Oh. Well, you could've stopped that a while ago." Chloe glanced at the bar. "She left early tonight."

Rachel spun and saw only Morgan at the bar, working it alone. "Why?"

"Maybe she wasn't feeling well? Maybe because of you?" Chloe gave her a soft smile. "I don't know for sure."

Rachel knew exactly how Blair was feeling because she felt the same. It was getting late, and the crowd had thinned quite a bit. "Are you sure she's not out back loading the van?" She usually did that around this time.

"No. I haven't seen her in a while. I'm pretty sure she's gone."

Rachel hadn't expected Blair to leave. She pushed by Chloe and sped to the bar.

"Red or white?" Morgan set a plastic wineglass on the bar.

"Water, please." Rachel had already drunk enough tonight.

Morgan set a bottle on the bar top. "Hey. I've been wanting to talk to you all night. I need to explain about what you overheard—about the bet."

Her stomach squeezed. "I know all about it. There's not much more to explain."

"There is." Morgan let out a sigh. "I know it's hard to believe, but I can be a real jerk sometimes." Morgan had confidence of steel.

"Seems Blair can be as well."

"That's just the thing. I make random bets all the time with her about me getting someone into bed. It's a stupid thing I do."

"That doesn't make the situation any better." Rachel turned to leave the bar.

"Wait. This isn't coming out the right way." Morgan blew out a breath. "I make the bets, not Blair. She never takes me up on them, and I've never seen her bet on any woman. She wouldn't do that. Especially not on you."

"I'm not sure I believe that. But go on." She would listen to Morgan's story but couldn't guarantee she would buy in.

"I'm serious." Morgan frowned. "When you showed up in Las Vegas, I was all ready to make all your dreams come true for a night." She really was full of herself.

"I don't recall having that much interaction with you."

"I remember that you were stressed. Your credit card wouldn't work for some reason, so I comped your drink that first night." Morgan paused to refill someone's glass with wine. "The next night Blair seemed to take an interest in you, which isn't something she does often with women who frequent the bar. She kind of took over, so I let her have you."

"So, you're saying she claimed me?" That wasn't much better than the bet.

"Jesus, no." Morgan clenched the edge of the bar. "She thought you were nice—said you were interesting. And then when you showed up at the winery the next day, I could see it was more than that."

"I didn't realize you two were that close."

"We weren't for a long time, but then after the Sophie-and-Tess thing, we moved to Vegas and rented a house together."

"Why Vegas?"

"She needed to get away and make some money, and I thought it would be a fun distraction from school. She had family there too, so it was a no-brainer."

She glanced around the room. "Where is Blair?"

"She left about an hour ago. Has an early appointment tomorrow."

That was unusual. What kind of an appointment could she possibly have that would prompt her to leave a job early? "What kind?" Here she was digging into Blair's business like it she was entitled to know, feeling indignant that she wasn't aware, even though she hadn't given Blair the opportunity to tell her anything in close to a week.

Morgan shrugged. "She didn't say."

"What about the bar? Is she just going to leave it here overnight?" Blair would probably never trust her equipment to anyone after she'd put so much money into it.

"She took an Uber, so I've got the van. I'll pack it up and drop it off tomorrow."

Rachel wanted to run outside and call Blair—find out what she was doing in the morning, what was so important—but she held steady and leaned against the bar. "So, what do you think I should do, Morgan? Just forget about what I heard you two discussing last week?"

"Yes." Morgan was emphatic. "I was only kidding with her." She shrugged. "I say stupid things just for fun. Please don't punish Blair for that."

"Thank you for telling me." She took in a deep breath and walked across the bar to where Shay and Chloe were standing watching her. Apparently, she was the last act of the night.

"You were at the bar an awfully long time." Shay smiled softly.

She nodded. "Talking to Morgan."

"What'd she say?" Shay seemed eager to find out more information.

"Morgan swears it was all her. It's some kind of game she plays."

Shay's smile widened. "So, Morgan made the bet and Blair never bought in?"

"That's what she said." She was beginning to believe her—believe them both.

"I think you just received your cue to make this whole misunderstanding go away."

"I agree." Chloe touched her shoulder. "You want it to. Don't you?"

She nodded. It had been a week since she'd overheard them talking. Blair had continued to send daily texts, and she'd had to force herself not to respond. She'd made a bad situation worse by simply avoiding it. Now she had to figure out why a simple misunderstanding could create such a big divide between them. Why *she'd* let it happen. The whole idea of committing to Blair terrified her for some reason. It wasn't about Shay any longer—she was never going to have her—and she really didn't want Shay anymore. Why was she so reluctant to resolve things with Blair?

CHAPTER THIRTY-ONE

B lair's stomach rumbled as she thought about seeing Rachel at the gallery event earlier tonight. Blair had glanced across the gallery, and her stomach had vaulted into a somersault. She hadn't been sure if Rachel would show tonight, considering their current situation. But there she was, avoiding eye contact. Her eyes were somewhat sunken, with dark circles below them. Evidently Rachel wasn't doing well with the separation either. Later, when she'd glanced around the gallery, she saw no sign of Rachel. Not that she would've talked to her anyway.

It had been a hell of a week. Rachel had been incommunicado, and seeing Rachel avoid her was just the topper on the cake. At this point she didn't know if they were still together, broken up, or on a break. Being in limbo hurt more than she'd ever imagined.

She screwed the top off a bottle of sparkling water and chugged as she settled into the queen-size bed in Tess and Sophie's spare room. She'd been grateful for their offer to let her stay until she found a new place. Downsizing her living arrangements was just the beginning of this new life journey. The past few days had been a whirlwind of stress and decisions she hadn't been ready to deal with, but now it was done. She was in a partnership with Paige McCormack and half owner of Sugar Bar. The change was exhilarating and terrifying all at once.

The opportunity to merge her business, Blissful Bubbles, with Cocktail City had been timely. Paige's proposition had been a good one. They would join forces to create a new business and work as partners to keep the market they'd shared while previously working independently. She couldn't refuse the offer since she'd been struggling to keep from going bankrupt the last few months.

Everything had happened so fast. The merger, the move, the breakup…was it really a breakup? She'd tried to contact Rachel again this morning, but she didn't respond. Rachel could be completely done with her. She had no clue, only a sick feeling in her stomach.

The soft knock on her door jarred her out of her thoughts. "Come in."

The door opened slightly, and Tess poked her head inside. "You okay?"

"I'm good."

Tess moved across the room and took a seat on the edge of the bed. "You're home early. Did you talk to Rachel tonight?"

She shook her head. "She was too busy with Shay. Didn't see much of her all night."

"That was probably more about avoiding you than about being with Shay."

"Maybe." She flattened the sheet across her waist. "I don't know what to do. I have so much going on right now, and she won't even talk to me." Heat burned her cheeks as tears began to fall. "I don't even know what to say to her."

Tess glanced at her phone on the nightstand. "Why don't I take this? If she calls, I'll wake you." She lifted her eyebrows. "Okay?"

"But—"

"No buts. You have a big day tomorrow. You need to get some rest."

Sophie came through the door and jumped onto the bottom of the bed. "Are we having a slumber party?"

"Tomorrow night. After we get this one's furniture moved into storage."

She rubbed the tears from her cheeks. "Thank you both so much for helping me. I don't know how I would've done it so quickly without you."

Tess squeezed her hand. "No thanks needed. That's what friends are for, right?" She glanced at Sophie.

Sophie nodded. "Besides, we owe you one or two for helping us figure things out."

"Yeah, you do." She smiled. Bringing Tess and Sophie together had been unintended and a bit confusing, but it had been the right thing to do.

Tess released her hand and stood before she reached for Sophie's. "Come on, love. We need to get some sleep as well, if we're going to be up bright and early to help."

Sophie slid off the bed and took Tess's hand before she moved to the door. "You have her phone?" They seemed to be conspiring to keep her silent tonight.

"I do. Get some rest. We'll wake you in the morning." Tess closed the door as she left the bedroom.

She would do her best to sleep, but she had no guarantees. Just like she hadn't had any for the past week.

Rachel had driven by Blair's house, but it was dark inside. Not even the flash of the TV lit up the curtains. She didn't seem to be home. Was she staying with someone else tonight? Had she moved on that quickly? She shook herself from the panic. That was ridiculous. Blair wouldn't do that. Not after everything they'd had together. Would she? Where was she?

She fiddled with the key Blair had given her. She could just go inside and see—talk to her like any normal adult would. Letting herself in at this point would be a bad idea though. She dropped the key into the console, walked to the door, and knocked lightly. No movement or sound inside. She rang the bell. Still nothing. Blair really wasn't home. She peeked through a slit in the curtains on the side window and spotted several large boxes in the living room, but it was too dark to really see anything. What the hell was going on?

She rushed to her car and found her phone. Blair had called again this morning, and she hadn't answered—hadn't listened to the voice mail either. She clicked the voice mail, and Blair's voice came through the speaker.

"Hey there. I know you don't want to talk to me right now, but I need to tell you about a couple of things, and I don't want to do it in a voice mail. So, will you call me back...please?"

"Fuck." She immediately hit the call-back button, but the phone went straight to voice mail. Where the hell was she? What did Blair need to tell her? She threw open the car door and rushed to the front door, phone in one hand and key in the other. She was determined to find out. The phone rang as she was trying to shove the key in the lock. It was Blair. "Where are you?"

"Hi, Rachel. It's Tess."

"Where's Blair?" Why was Tess answering her phone? Was she hurt? Terror hit her immediately. "Is she okay?"

"She's fine. She's asleep here at my house."

"Why do you have her phone?"

"Listen. It's been a long week, and she has a big day tomorrow." Tess was short with her, clearly annoyed.

"What are you talking about?" She walked back to her car.

Tess blew a breath through the speaker. "I thought she called you...several times."

"She did, but apparently she didn't want to leave a message about whatever's happening tomorrow, so can you clue me in?"

"No. She should tell you." Tess wasn't budging.

"Oh my God. Is it something serious? Is she sick?"

"No. It's nothing with her health." Tess's voice was slow and even. "We'll be at her house around seven in the morning. Why don't come by and talk to her?"

Nothing like forcing her to see Blair by not telling her anything. "Okay. I'll do that." What was so secret that Tess couldn't tell her— didn't want to tell her?

"For what it's worth, Rach, she really does care about you. Stop being an ass and remember that when you see her in the morning." Tess didn't pull any punches.

"I never doubted that. I just needed time to digest what happened." She'd probably taken more time to get over it than she should've, but now she was unsure about everything.

"I'm glad to hear that, because she really needs you right now. You, of all people, should be there for her."

Again with the vague reference. "I'll see you in the morning." She hit the end button. She didn't know what the hell was going on, but even if she was still mixed up about everything, she sure wasn't ready to let Blair go.

CHAPTER THIRTY-TWO

When Rachel turned onto Blair's street, her neck burned at the sight of the small moving truck in the driveway and a couple of guys loading furniture. *She's moving—without even telling me?* What was happening to her life? It was all slipping away too quickly. She hadn't made any long-term plans with anyone since she'd fallen for Shay, but now that she'd been with Blair, she couldn't imagine spending her life with anyone else.

The car jolted as she pulled up to the curb, threw it into park, and killed the engine. She almost tripped on the threshold as she raced into the house. "Blair?" She raced down the hallway to the bedroom. All the furniture was gone—loaded into the truck. "Blair," she shouted as she raced into the kitchen. Not there either. She pushed through the door into the garage, where the garage door was open to the street now. Blair seemed to have noticed her car and was walking toward it.

She stopped and caught her breath. "Hey there." What a stupid thing to say after she'd ignored her all week.

Blair spun around but didn't smile as she strolled up the driveway. "You're here."

"I came by last night, but you weren't home."

"I was at Tess and Sophie's."

"I know. I called when I couldn't find you."

"Right." Blair glanced up at the sky. "Tess took my phone."

"I know I've been a shit this week—not returning your calls, your texts. We had a new batch of interns start." Supervising the new interns was exhausting, but that was no excuse.

"You're fine." Blair reached for her, took her hands. "I know you needed time to sort it all out." Her forehead creased, and she took in a deep breath. "I hope that's done."

It was and it wasn't. "What the hell is going on here? Why are you moving?"

"I've been struggling with the cost of this place and decided to downsize. Maybe get a one-bedroom in a less ritzy neighborhood."

"Move in with me." The words whooshed out of Rachel's mouth before she could stop them. She was being impulsive and hadn't thought it through at all, but her heart was leading now.

"I'm not sure that's a good idea, with the way things are between us now." Blair's smile faded. "Tess and Sophie said I can stay with them until I find something." She released her hands and turned to go inside.

"Wait." She caught Blair by the arm. "I've thought a lot about what you and I have together—and what I want." She let go of Blair's arm and backed up. She needed to get her thoughts straight, and she couldn't do that with Blair standing so close.

"I never intended to hurt you." Blair's eyes were wide, searching, a touch of moisture beginning to fill them.

"Just listen. Please." She wasn't going to be able to say anything if she didn't do it now. "I'm not perfect. I don't think things through. I make bad assumptions and do shitty things because of them. I know Morgan made the bet, not you. She confirmed that last night." She kept eye contact—forcing herself to watch the tears stream down Blair's face. "She was the last of several people to tell me what an idiot I've been." *Such an idiot.*

Blair moved closer. "You're not an idiot." Blair brushed the moisture from her own face.

"Yeah. I am. If I wasn't, I would've told you some things a long time ago."

"What things?" Blair's eyes were a bright, glistening green.

"I've been floundering for so long in an impossible situation— waiting for someone who doesn't love me. Then you came along and changed everything." Rachel's voice cracked. "When I visualize my forever now, you're the one I see—no one else, and I can't seem to erase that image. I don't want to." Tears began to flow across her cheeks, and she couldn't stop the sobs that came next. The reality hit hard—losing Blair would devastate her.

Blair slipped her arms around her and held her tightly. Then they were both sobbing. They stayed like that for what seemed like hours but was only minutes. The comfort of Blair holding her, rubbing her back as she got a grip and settled herself was a clear sign that this was meant to be. She looked into Blair's eyes and saw bloodshot happiness in them, if that was even a real thing. The kiss that came next began urgently and quickly morphed into a long, slow, sweetness that she'd missed so much over the past week. She could never let Blair go—not over some stupid misunderstanding or her own irrational insecurities.

When the kiss ended, Blair put her forehead to hers and stared into her eyes. "I'm glad you told me. I can't see myself with anyone else either."

She took Blair's face into her hands and kissed her again—tentatively, softly, and slowly.

Blair pressed her lips to hers one last time. "I need to tell you something else." She seemed nervous, which made Rachel nervous as well. "You already know I made some financial decisions about my living arrangements this week, but I also decided something about my business."

"Do you need money? I'll give you whatever you need."

Blair smiled. "Thank you for that, but no. I made an agreement with Paige from Cocktail City."

"What? Why her?" *And not me? Because you've been fucking MIA for the past week, idiot.*

"She proposed something that made a lot of sense. Working with only Morgan, I've been struggling with running the financials as well as working the hours. I can't do it all. Paige has a large crew, which also means a large payroll, and I was taking enough of her market share to impact her business. Neither of us can make it on our own, so we're starting a new business venture together and calling it Sugar Bar."

"I wish you'd told me sooner. I could've helped."

"I know, but then we both would've been stressed even more. Everything still would've been on me to make the business work. This way, Paige and I will be partners. We'll keep her staff and Morgan, if she wants to stay on, which means we'll share the load, and I won't have to work as much."

"Will you be happy in a partnership with Paige? I mean, you wanted to have *your own* business."

"I did, but it's too much work without help from someone else who knows the ropes. Plus, I want to be able to enjoy time with you without worrying about it."

"Sugar Bar. I like that."

"I thought you would."

"So, will you move in with me?" Blair didn't have a reason not to now. All those doubts were gone—she hoped.

"Yeah. I will." Blair grinned. "I need someone to binge-watch TV with. Tess and Sophie watch some *weird* stuff. Not anything we like."

"What's wrong with them?" Rachel kissed her long and slow—the kind of kiss that could last for a thousand years.

"It's about time you showed up." Tess glared at Rachel as she walked up the driveway into the garage. "If you love someone, you show up. It's how you tell those you care about that you *actually do care*—during *highs and lows*. You don't just ignore their calls and texts." Tess was angry—hotter than Blair had ever seen her, not even giving either of them a chance to speak. "And if you don't forgive her this very minute, you don't deserve her." She propped a hand on her hip.

"It's okay." Blair moved between them quickly and took Tess by the shoulders. "We talked. We're good."

"You are?" Tess raised her eyebrows as she glanced at Rachel and then back at her. "You told her everything?"

Blair nodded and smiled. "I did. I told her everything that's happened this week."

Rachel wrapped her arms around Blair's waist as she peered over her shoulder at Tess. "She did, and I've asked Blair to move in with me."

Tess's face went blank. "Oh. Well. Then I guess I didn't need to give that speech."

"No. You did." Rachel moved next to Blair and took her hand. "You're absolutely right. I was MIA when I should've been with Blair helping her through all this." She glanced at Blair. "I'm sorry for that."

Sophie appeared from the car and came up the driveway. "Looks like we're all good here, right?" She entered the garage. Blair hadn't known she'd even come. Must have been on a call. "So, let's finish getting you moved out of this place." Sophie continued into the house, and Tess followed.

Rachel held steady as she moved to the door. "Wait. I need to tell you something." She looked serious.

"Okay." Blair scrunched her eyebrows together.

"What Tess said about forgiving you wasn't exactly right. You didn't do anything wrong. I know that now. I'm the one who needs to ask for forgiveness. I should've contacted you sooner—let you explain—believed you—and I'm sorry I didn't."

Blair took Rachel's face in her hands and kissed her. "You're forgiven." And just like that, all was right in her world again.

Rachel had instructed the movers to transport all of Blair's belongings to her house. Some had ended up in the garage until they could find a place inside or decide about which pieces of furniture would stay and which would be sold or go into storage.

Standing back, she looked at the new living-room arrangement and felt good—settled even—about it all. She hadn't felt that way in a very long time.

Blair came out of the bedroom. "What's wrong?" She'd changed into pajama pants and a T-shirt, and her hair was all mussed around her face.

"Nothing." She shook her head. Absolutely nothing was wrong in her life right now, and it felt weird.

"Are you sure? You look a bit shell-shocked."

"I think I am." She held out her hands at the new assortment of furniture. "This isn't what I expected."

Blair's smile faded. "Oh."

"I mean, I didn't expect it all to be so easy." She shook her head at her own misgivings. "You, me, this. Everything feels right." She didn't doubt that she was exactly where she should be.

Blair crossed the room and took her in her arms. "Really?"

"Absolutely." She kissed her and enjoyed the familiarity of Blair's tongue as it glided into her mouth, her arms pulling her closer, her everything pressed softly against her. Blair was home to her now.

EPILOGUE

Rachel couldn't stop grinning as she stood under the tallest section of the Stardust sign in the Neon Boneyard. She knew of much fancier places to get married in Las Vegas, but this spot was special to her and to Blair. Most people would say this setting was kind of corny for a wedding. In fact, not too long ago Rachel would've said the same. The park had a different section for elopements, but it turned out that Blair *really did* know a guy and had arranged to hold the ceremony under the sign where they first began to fall in love. She'd realized after that kiss in the park that she'd wanted to be with Blair, but she just couldn't admit it to herself until Blair had shown up in her life again in Florida. The probability of love coming from a chance meeting in Las Vegas had been slim, but they'd played the odds and won.

Shay laced her fingers in Rachel's and clasped her hand. "You ready for this?"

"Absolutely." She looked up over her shoulder at the huge star-shaped sign thrusting far into the air and shivered. It was majestic, to say the least.

Sophie stood on Rachel's other side and stared up at it. "At first I didn't understand why you picked this spot, but now I can see why. This sign is magnificent in the dark." They'd arrived at dusk, before the vibrant pastel colors had shown themselves.

When they'd decided to get married, they wanted it to happen as soon as possible. So they'd kept the event small, inviting only Shay, Chloe, Tess, Sophie, and Morgan, although she had opted out of the couples weekend. Their parents would be disappointed that they'd eloped, but she and Blair wanted the ceremony to be done the way they envisioned it—here in this special place. Involving both mothers of the brides would make that plan difficult. They would have a reception the following month, and both moms would have a say in how and where that happened.

They'd had a few hurdles to jump within their timeline. Tess had volunteered to officiate, which was no simple task. She'd had to apply in Clark County, take an online course to determine eligibility, fill out an application packet, and provide a notarized character reference from both Rachel and Blair. Getting the license was the easiest task of all. They'd picked it up from the Clark County Marriage License Bureau the day before. The main holdup in timing was that Tess had to file her application thirty days before the ceremony. Fortunately, it had been approved within a couple of weeks, so they had moved all their plans forward to make the wedding happen sooner.

As Chloe walked down the pathway and took her place next to Shay, strangers gathered on the other side of the pathway to watch like they'd all been invited to the wedding event of the season. When Rachel glimpsed Blair dressed in a gorgeous, knee-length, fitted sheath dress overlaid with a section of art-deco-inspired silvery sequins down the middle, her stomach tingled. Fancy and feminine, just like Blair. Her gorgeous, tanned arms peeked out under the sleeveless silhouette. They'd chosen the day's outfits together—first Blair's dress and then Rachel's bateau-neck, floor-length chiffon, sleeveless, layered lace pantsuit and jacket. They were destined to be the chatter topic of all the uninvited guests for days.

Blair smiled widely as she strolled toward them, accompanied by Tess. Rachel's heart pounded, and Shay seemed to notice. Shay squeezed Rachel's hand as though Shay was afraid she might bolt. Rachel was nervous, but not from fear this time. She was in love and never again wanted to suppress this wonderful feeling. The only thing that could top this moment was having Blair in her arms as her wife when the ceremony ended. That couldn't happen soon enough.

Blair stared into Rachel's eyes as she began reciting her vows. "From the first moment we met I knew we had something special. No-frills entertainment and fabulous sex." Blair grinned. "I felt hopeless when you left this city—thought I'd never see you again." Tears began to well in Blair's eyes. "And then you reappeared in my life out of nowhere, and I knew we were meant to be." She chuckled. "You took some convincing, but you eventually bought in." She squeezed Rachel's hands. "And now I've won the best jackpot in Vegas. I have you and will love you each and every day we have together."

That was Rachel's cue. "I was unsure—not of you, but of myself. Unsure I could commit without doubt, without knowing what the future might hold. But I see it now, and I know it's with you—I can't imagine a tomorrow without you. I can't see anything clearly without you in my life. So, if you'll have me, I promise not to doubt or run ever again, and to love you for the rest of my life." The heat from her tears burned her cheeks. She'd sworn she wouldn't cry, but she'd lost the battle.

Blair took her into her arms and whispered, "I promise never to let anyone gamble on our love again."

Tess cleared her throat. "With the power vested in me, I pronounce you joined in marriage." She glanced at Blair and then at Rachel. "You may kiss your bride."

And Rachel did just that—kissed Blair with the intensity of all their kisses combined—filled with love, passion, and excitement for their new journey together...for as long as they both shall live.

THE END

About the Author

Dena Blake grew up in a small town just north of San Francisco where she learned to play softball, ride motorcycles, and grow vegetables. She eventually moved with her family to the Southwest where she began creating vivid characters in her mind and bringing them to life on paper.

Dena currently lives in the Southwest with her partner and is constantly amazed at what she learns from her two children. She is a would-be chef, tech nerd, and occasional auto mechanic who has a weakness for dark chocolate and a good cup of coffee.

Books Available from Bold Strokes Books

A Champion for Tinker Creek by D.C. Robeline. Lyle James has rescued his dad's auto repair business, but when city hall condemns his neighborhood, Lyle learns only trusting will save his life and help him find love. (978-1-63679-213-2)

Closed-Door Policy by Erin Zak. Going back to college is never easy, but Caroline Stevens is prepared to work hard and change her life for the better. What she's not prepared for is Dr. Atlanta Morris, her gorgeous new professor. (978-1-63679-181-4)

Homeworld by Gun Brooke. Headed by Captain Holly Crowe, the spaceship Velocity's crew journeys toward their alien ancestors' homeworld, and what they find is completely unexpected—and they're not safe. (978-1-63679-177-7)

Outland by Kristin Keppler & Allisa Bahney. Danielle Clark and Katelyn Turner can't seem to stay away from one another even as the war for the wastelands tests their loyalty to each other and to their people. (978-1-63679-154-8)

Secret Sanctuary by Nance Sparks. US Deputy Marshal Alex Trenton specializes in protecting those awaiting trial, but when danger threatens the woman she's falling for, Alex is in for the fight of her life. (978-1-63679-148-7)

Stranded Hearts by Kris Bryant, Amanda Radley, Emily Smith. In these novellas from award-winning authors, fate intervenes on behalf of love when characters are unexpectedly stuck together. With too much time and an irresistible attraction, anything could happen. (978-1-63679-182-1)

The Last Lavender Sister by Melissa Brayden. Aster Lavender sells her gourmet doughnuts and keeps a low profile; she never plans on the town's temporary veterinarian swooping in and making her feel like anything but a wallflower. (978-1-63679-130-2)

The Probability of Love by Dena Blake. As Blair and Rachel keep ending up in the same place despite the odds, can a one-night stand turn into forever? Or will the bet Blair never intended to make ruin their happily ever after? (978-1-63679-188-3)

Worth a Fortune by Sam Ledel. After placing a want ad for a personal secretary, a New York heiress is surprised when the woman who got away is the one interested in the position. (978-1-63679-175-3)

A Fox in Shadow by Jane Fletcher. Cassie's mission is to add new territory to the Kavillian empire—murder, betrayal, war, and the clash of cultures ensue. (978-1-63679-142-5)

Embracing the Moon by Jeannie Levig. Just as Gwen and Taylor are exploring the new love they've found, the present and past collide, threatening the future they long to share. (978-1-63555-462-5)

Forever Comes in Threes by D. Jackson Leigh. Efficiency expert Perry Chandler's ordered life is upended when she inherits three busy terriers, and the woman she's referred to for help turns out to be her bitter podcast rival, the very sexy Dr. Ming Lee. (978-1-63679-169-2)

Heckin' Lewd: Trans and Nonbinary Erotica by Mx. Nillin Lore. If you want smutty, fearless, gender-diverse erotica written by affirming own-voices folks who get it, then this is the book you've been looking for! (978-1-63679-240-8)

Missed Conception by Joy Argento. Maggie Walsh wants a relationship with Cassidy, the daughter she's only just discovered she has due to an in vitro mix-up. Heat kindles between Maggie and Cassidy's mother in a way neither expects. (978-1-63679-146-3)

Private Equity by Elle Spencer. Cassidy Bennett spends an unexpected evening at a lesbian nightclub with her notoriously reserved and demanding boss, Julia. After seeing a different side of Julia, Cassidy can't seem to shake her desire to know more. (978-1-63679-180-7)

Racing the Dawn by Sandra Barrett. After narrowly escaping a house fire, vampire Jade Murphy is unexpectedly intrigued by gorgeous firefighter Beth Jenssen, and her undead existence might just be perking up a bit. (978-1-63679-271-2)

Reclaiming Love by Amanda Radley. Sarah's tiny white lie means somehow convincing Pippa to pretend to be her girlfriend. Only the more time they spend faking it, the more real it feels. (978-1-63679-144-9)

Sol Cycle by Kimberly Cooper Griffin. An encounter in a park brings Ang and Krista together, but when Ang's attempts to help Krista go spectacularly wrong, their passion for each other might not be enough. (978-1-63679-137-1)

Trial and Error by Carsen Taite. Attorney Franco Rossi and Judge Nina Aguilar's reunion is fraught with courtroom conflict, undeniable chemistry, and danger. (978-1-63555-863-0)

A Long Way to Fall by Elle Spencer. A ski lodge, two strong-willed women, and a family feud that brings them together, but will it also tear them apart? (978-1-63679-005-3)

Barnabas Bopwright Saves the City by J. Marshall Freeman. When he uncovers a terror plot to destroy the city he loves, 15-year-old Barnabas Bopwright realizes it's up to him to save his home and bring deadly secrets into the light before it's too late. (978-1-63679-152-4)

Forever by Kris Bryant. When Savannah Edwards is invited to be the next bachelorette on the dating show When Sparks Fly, she'll show the world that finding true love on television can happen. (978-1-63679-029-9)

Ice on Wheels by Aurora Rey. All's fair in love and roller derby. That's Riley Fauchet's motto, until a new job lands her at the same company—and on the same team—as her rival Brooke Landry, the frosty jammer for the Big Easy Bruisers. (978-1-63679-179-1)

Inherit the Lightning by Bud Gundy. Darcy O'Brien and his sisters learn they are about to inherit an immense fortune, but a family mystery about to unravel after seventy years threatens to destroy everything. (978-1-63679-199-9)

Perfect Rivalry by Radclyffe. Two women set out to win the same career-making goal, but it's love that may turn out to be the final prize. (978-1-63679-216-3)

Something to Talk About by Ronica Black. Can quiet ranch owner Corey Durand give up her peaceful life and allow her feisty new neighbor into her heart? Or will past loss, present suitors, and town gossip ruin a long-awaited chance at love? (978-1-63679-114-2)

With a Minor in Murder by Karis Walsh. In the world of academia, police officer Clare Sawyer and professor Libby Hart team up to solve a murder. (978-1-63679-186-9)

Writer's Block by Ali Vali. Wyatt and Hayley might be made for each other if only they can get through nosy neighbors, the historic society, at-odds future plans, and all the secrets hidden in Wyatt's walls. (978-1-63679-021-3)

Cold Blood by Genevieve McCluer. Maybe together, Kalila and Dorenia have a chance of taking down the vampires who have eluded them all these years. And maybe, in each other, they can find a love worth living for. (978-1-63679-195-1)

Greener Pastures by Aurora Rey. When city girl and CPA Audrey Adams finds herself tending her aunt's farm, will Rowan Marshall—the charming cider maker next door—turn out to be her saving grace or the bane of her existence? (978-1-63679-116-6)

Grounded by Amanda Radley. For a second chance, Olivia and Emily will need to accept their mistakes, learn to communicate properly, and with a little help from five-year-old Henry, fall madly in love all over again. Sequel to Flight SQA016. (978-1-63679-241-5)

Journey's End by Amanda Radley. In this heartwarming conclusion to the Flight series, Olivia and Emily must finally decide what they want, what they need, and how to follow the dreams of their hearts. (978-1-63679-233-0)

Pursued: Lillian's Story by Felice Picano. Fleeing a disastrous marriage to the Lord Exchequer of England, Lillian of Ravenglass reveals an incident-filled, often bizarre, tale of great wealth and power, perfidy, and betrayal. (978-1-63679-197-5)

Secret Agent by Michelle Larkin. CIA agent Peyton North embarks on a global chase to apprehend rogue agent Zoey Blackwood, but her commitment to the mission is tested as the sparks between them ignite and their sizzling attraction approaches a point of no return. (978-1-63555-753-4)

Something Between Us by Krystina Rivers. A decade after her heart was broken under Don't Ask, Don't Tell, Kirby runs into her first love and has to decide if what's still between them is enough to heal her broken heart. (978-1-63679-135-7)

Sugar Girl by Emma L McGeown. Having traded in traditional romance for the perks of Sugar Dating, Ciara Reilly not only enjoys the no-strings-attached arrangement, she's also a hit with her clients. That is until she meets the beautiful entrepreneur Charlie Keller who makes her want to go sugar-free. (978-1-63679-156-2)

The Business of Pleasure by Ronica Black. Editor in chief Valerie Raffield is quickly becoming smitten by Lennox, the graphic artist she's hired to work remotely. But when Lennox doesn't show for their first face-to-face meeting, Valerie's heart and her business may be in jeopardy. (978-1-63679-134-0)

The Hummingbird Sanctuary by Erin Zak. The Hummingbird Sanctuary, Colorado's hottest resort destination: Come for the mountains, stay for the charm, and enjoy the drama as Olive, Eleanor, and Harriet figure out the meaning of true friendship. (978-1-63679-163-0)

The Witch Queen's Mate by Jennifer Karter. Barra and Silvi must overcome their ingrained hatred and prejudice to use Barra's magic and save both their peoples, not just from slavery, but destruction. (978-1-63679-202-6)

With a Twist by Georgia Beers. Starting over isn't easy for Amelia Martini. When the irritatingly cheerful Kirby Dupress comes into her life will Amelia be brave enough to go after the love she really wants? (978-1-63555-987-3)

Business of the Heart by Claire Forsythe. When a hopeless romantic meets a tough-as-nails cynic, they'll need to overcome the wounds of the past to discover that their hearts are the most important business of all. (978-1-63679-167-8)

Dying for You by Jenny Frame. Can Victorija Dred keep an age-old vow and fight the need to take blood from Daisy Macdougall? (978-1-63679-073-2)

Exclusive by Melissa Brayden. Skylar Ruiz lands the TV reporting job of a lifetime, but is she willing to sacrifice it all for the love of her longtime crush, anchorwoman Carolyn McNamara? (978-1-63679-112-8)

Her Duchess to Desire by Jane Walsh. An up-and-coming interior designer seeks to create a happily ever after with an intriguing duchess, proving that love never goes out of fashion. (978-1-63679-065-7)

Murder on Monte Vista by David S. Pederson. Private Detective Mason Adler's angst at turning fifty is forgotten when his "birthday present," the handsome, young Henry Bowtrickle, turns up dead, and it's up to Mason to figure out who did it, and why. (978-1-63679-124-1)

Take Her Down by Lauren Emily Whalen. Stakes are cutthroat, scheming is creative, and loyalty is ever-changing in this queer, female-driven YA retelling of Shakespeare's Julius Caesar. (978-1-63679-089-3)

The Game by Jan Gayle. Ryan Gibbs is a talented golfer, but her guilt means she may never leave her small town, even if Katherine Reese tempts her with competition and passion. (978-1-63679-126-5)

Whereabouts Unknown by Meredith Doench. While homicide detective Theodora Madsen recovers from a potentially career-ending injury, she scrambles to solve the cases of two missing sixteen-year-old girls from Ohio. (978-1-63555-647-6)